"Why are you leaving, Darcy?"

"The longer I've stayed—maybe I've overstayed—the more lost I feel." She averted her eyes. "Perhaps it's time for me to see if there's more out there."

"Does more have to be out there? Not here?"

Her gaze returned to his. "I thought you'd understand, Jax. We're both all-or-nothing people."

"You want to know the real reason I didn't return until now?" His heart drummed in his chest. "I didn't think there could ever be a place here for me again."

"But you're home now, Jax."

"Am I?" He studied her. "Will you forgive me, Darcy?"

His question was about so much more than what happened this afternoon.

She looked at him. "I'm here, aren't I?"

"Can we get back to being friends?" He thrust out his chin. "We were friends, Darcy. Once."

"Trust might be trickier than merely coming home."

Jax tightened his jaw. "A chance is all I'm asking."

Lisa Carter and her family make their home in
North Carolina. In addition to her Love Inspired
novels, she writes romantic suspense for Abingdon
Press. When she isn't writing, Lisa enjoys traveling
to romantic locales, teaching writing workshops
and researching her next exotic adventure.
She has strong opinions on barbecue and ACC
basketball. She loves to hear from readers.
Connect with Lisa at lisacarterauthor.com.

Books by Lisa Carter

Love Inspired

Coast Guard Courtship
Coast Guard Sweetheart
Falling for the Single Dad
The Deputy's Perfect Match
The Bachelor's Unexpected Family
The Christmas Baby
Hometown Reunion

Hometown Reunion

Lisa Carter

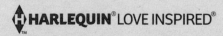

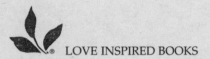

LOVE INSPIRED BOOKS

ISBN-13: 978-1-335-42808-0

Hometown Reunion

Copyright © 2018 by Lisa Carter

www.Harlequin.com

Printed in U.S.A.

Come unto me, all ye that labour and are heavy laden, and I will give you rest. Take my yoke upon you, and learn of me; for I am meek and lowly in heart: and ye shall find rest unto your souls. For my yoke is easy, and my burden is light.
—*Matthew* 11:28–30

This book is dedicated to Daniel
and Debbie Riley. Thanks so much for
your friendship. And even after all these years,
a special thank you for still making me feel
at home every time I visit the Eastern Shore.

Chapter One

Stepping out of his Ford 250, Jaxon Pruitt winced as his knees creaked. At thirty-two, he was already nothing but a washed-up old man. A failure.

He glanced at his two-year-old son, Brody, strapped in his car seat. Correction—Jax was a washed-up, thirty-two-year-old *dad*.

After all these years, he was back where he'd begun, at Kiptohanock Kayaking. The shop was on the seawall, sandwiched between the marine animal hospital and the Coast Guard station.

From the adjacent harbor, a slight breeze wafted. Recreational and commercial fishing boats bobbed in the marina. And the once familiar scent of briny seawater filled his nostrils. At the sound of a loud caw, both he and Brody looked skyward. Overhead, a seagull performed an acrobatic figure eight.

As Jax reached to unbuckle the harness, Brody shrank into the seat. The toddler's brown eyes went wide, piercing Jax's heart. A former Green Beret, he'd always known what to do on any given mission, but Jax didn't know how to fix things with the son he barely knew.

He had no clue how to be not just a father, but *Brody's* father. He'd messed up everything with Adrienne, and now he had no idea how to help Brody deal with her loss.

Brody closed his eyes and stuck his thumb into his mouth. With a click, Jax released the seat buckle, and Brody's eyes popped open. But the thumb remained in his mouth. Giving the child space, Jax backed away. His work boots crunched on the crushed-shell parking lot.

Seizing his chance, Brody scrambled out of the crew cab like a convict desperate to escape Alcatraz. Despite short toddler legs, he jumped to the ground in a move that made his airborne-qualified father proud.

But those days were behind Jax. He fought the urge to give in to the despair dogging him since his commanding officer had pulled him aside to deliver the life-changing news of his wife's death.

"Wanna go home," Brody whispered.

Jax wanted to go home, too. If only he knew where home resided. That was the reason he'd brought his son to the small fishing village in seaside Virginia where he'd grown up.

Was this a giant mistake? A ten-year combat veteran, he hadn't called any place home in a long time. And with Adrienne gone, perhaps home was a place that no longer existed for him.

So far, the transition from military to civilian life had been anything but smooth sailing. Thank God for his aunt, and the new start she offered him.

Kiptohanock Kayaking was an opportunity to make a home for Brody. Maybe Jax's last chance to bond with his son. If it wasn't already too late.

He shook himself. He couldn't afford pessimism. As a former member of the elite Special Forces, he was trained to never quit. And no matter what it took, whatever sacrifice, he'd make this work with Brody. Their survival as a family depended on it.

Per his training, Jax scoped out the terrain. On this mid-June Saturday, two vehicles were parked outside the outfitters shop. A seen-better-days bronze SUV with an empty roof rack, and next to it, his aunt's burgundy Grand Cherokee.

A bell jangled as his aunt stepped out of the shop onto the porch. Grinning, she waved them over. A lot had happened in his life since he'd worked here during high-school summers. More than the years or mileage would indicate.

He took Brody's small hand. "Let's go meet Aunt Shirley." He towed his son toward the porch.

After spending a disastrous six months with Adrienne's family, Jax found it good to see a friendly face. In cargo pants and the buttoned-up sleeves of her quick-dry shirt, his aunt was a walking advertisement for an outdoor provision company. Only these days, her hair was more salt than the pepper he remembered.

Dropping his hold on Brody, Jax engulfed her in a bear-size hug. The sheen of tears in the eyes of his unsentimental, take-no-prisoners relative surprised him.

"You haven't changed a bit." She clapped Jax on the back, jolting him. At six foot three, he wasn't easy to jolt. "A little taller, certainly broader in the shoulders." Her twinkling blue eyes teased him. "Far more handsome, if that's possible."

For the first time since driving over the Bay Bridge Tunnel from the mainland, he smiled. "And you are eternally youthful."

"Not true, but thank you." She gave him a wry smile in return. "I like to think I've mellowed with age."

"Aunt Shirley, this is my son, Brody."

Hunkered near the railing, Brody turned his little mouth upside down.

Jax bit off a sigh. "Brody, come meet Aunt Shirley. We'll be living at her old house."

Brody's brows drew together like two wiggly caterpillars. *"No."* His favorite word.

"I see the resemblance in the scowl." Shirley blew out a breath. "Is he as stubborn and mule-headed as you've always been, dear nephew?"

Scrubbing his hand over his face, he laughed.

Blunt as always. The more things changed, the more they stayed the same.

"He's got Pruitt blood in him. Won't take long for him to fall hopelessly in love with Shore life." She winked. "You, too."

Jax felt hopeless, though not with love. Time had run out for him and Adrienne. The enormous responsibility of being a single parent weighed heavy on his not-feeling-so-broad shoulders.

"I'm grateful for this lifeline you've thrown me, Aunt Shirl."

Like a swift kick in the pants, she poked him with her bony elbow. "So don't blow it, soldier."

His lips twitched. His maiden aunt would've made an excellent drill sergeant.

Shirley squeezed his arm. "Darcy's not happy about our arrangement. She's not exactly your biggest fan."

He grunted. "I can always count on you to give it to me straight, Aunt Shirl."

The short bark of her laugh echoed over the tidal estuary behind the shop. "But I've no doubt with that renowned Pruitt charm of yours, you'll find a way to convince her to stay for the busy summer season."

His so-called charm was his fallback position. As comfortable as a broken-in, well-loved baseball glove. Where he kept his feelings safely hidden.

Jax made a face. "The way I remember it, Darcy

Parks doesn't charm easily. Or maybe she's just immune to mine."

"Nothing worth having is ever easy."

"I'm prepared to give the business everything I've got." He frowned. "We are talking about the business, right?"

Shirley stuck her tongue in her cheek. "Don't tell your brothers I said so, but you're my favorite Pruitt nephew. I have full confidence in your ability to handle every challenge that comes your way."

"Like fiscal management?"

"That, too." Her eyes sparkled. "It's good to have you home, Jaxon."

With his face pressed between the railing spindles, Brody peered out over the village green. Like a prisoner through iron bars.

She tossed Jax a ring of keys. He caught them with one hand.

His aunt plodded down the wooden steps in her hiking boots. "How about I take this little sea urchin over to the Sandpiper Café for some Long John doughnuts before they close this afternoon?"

In true Tidewater fashion, her "about" came out sounding like "a boot." The soft musicality of her speech brought an unexpected welling to his eyes. It had been a long time since he'd been among his own people on the Eastern Shore. Too long.

Brody let go of the railing. "Hungwy."

She smirked. "You trying to starve this growing boy, Jaxon?"

"We had a burger at the Bay Bridge Grill for lunch." He squared his shoulders. "Shakes, too."

One of the few things he knew about kids: keep feeding them so they don't turn on you.

She held her hand out to Brody. "Ready?"

He snatched his hands behind his back. "No."

Jax gasped. "Brody…"

His aunt widened her stance. "Do you want doughnuts or not, young man? Makes me no never mind, either way."

Brody jerked his thumb in Jax's direction. *"Him?"*

Not once since Adrienne died had Brody called him Daddy. Most of the time, he refused to communicate with Jax at all. Except for *no*. He'd mastered that word.

"Your dad will be waiting right here when we get back." She patted Brody's shoulder. An awkward "I don't know what to do with a child" pat.

Join the club. He didn't, either.

"I'll be here, I promise, Brody."

His son glared at him. An indication of what he thought of his father's promises?

"Just like you." Shirley chuckled. "In so many hardheaded, annoying ways…"

Great. Just great. He rubbed the back of his neck.

"Darcy's on the dock. You two best get reacquainted." A strange smile flitted across Shirley's lips. "Welcome home, Jaxon. To the first day of the rest of your life."

Jax swallowed. *I know we haven't talked in a while, but please, God, make it so.*

With visible reluctance, Brody took her hand. As they walked toward the diner down the street, his dark head swiveled for one last glimpse of his father.

Like Adrienne that last day before they'd both deployed on separate assignments, never to see each other again. Jax's lungs constricted. Guilt cutting off his air supply.

In a single bound, he came off the porch and rounded the corner of the shop. His legs ate up the ground, past the stacked kayaks and paddles. Dodging the pile of orange lifejackets.

Leaping onto the wooden planks, he felt the dock shudder beneath his weight. But spotting the silhouette of a woman sitting on the far end, he came to an abrupt halt.

Midafternoon, the sun arced high in the cerulean sky. The cove glimmered like a treasure chest filled with glistening diamonds. Her legs dangled over the water, but in one lithe motion, she rose. And bathed in golden light, she faced him.

His heart sped up. "Darcy?"

She bridged the distance between them on the dock. And he got his first good look at her in over a decade. She hadn't changed much.

His breathing slowed. Somehow he'd been afraid she had. To him, Darcy was summer sunshine. Like the shimmery light playing across the pearlescent string of the barrier islands.

A sea breeze lifted a silky wave of the strawberry blonde hair skimming her shoulder. Freckles still sprinkled her nose. Her sun-kissed tan reflected the beach girl she was and had always been.

Darcy Parks, the little tomboy who lived next door to the Pruitts. Athletically slim, but rounded with more womanly curves than the sixteen-year-old he'd known. But like him, older.

Her blue-green eyes—like many here on the Shore—reflected the cool depths of the Machipongo Inlet. Becoming aware of her appraising scrutiny, he stuffed his hands in his pockets, striving for a nonchalance he didn't feel.

Full of an untried optimism, he'd joined the army right out of high school to fight global terrorism. And his success or failure now depended on the grown-up version of a girl he'd once possessed a great fondness for.

Eyes flashing, she raised her chin. "Long time no see, Jaxon." She shouldered past him toward the store.

His defenses climbed. Not the same girl he remembered. His mistake. He followed Darcy into the shop. Not the welcome he hoped for.

But after how he'd left things between them the day he reported for Basic, probably the welcome he deserved.

She'd been robbed.

Though perhaps not in a literal sense. And robbery wasn't even the worst of it.

Inside the outfitters shop, Darcy glowered at her best friend's older brother. "Nepotism doesn't become you, Jaxon."

Jax leaned one hip against the nearest available surface. Shirley's desk. Soon to be his.

Her fingers curled against her thighs. The leaning drove Darcy crazy. Always had.

When they were children, Jax had leaned against the oak tree, straddling their adjoining backyards. In high school, after football drills, he'd leaned against the gymnasium wall to watch his sister, Anna, and Darcy during volleyball practice.

Leaning. Always leaning. Had the military taught him nothing? Was the ex-Green Beret incapable of standing upright?

He cocked his head. "Don't make this more than it was. A simple business transaction, Darce. Nothing more."

She bristled. "Don't call me Darce."

Not only had she lost the chance to buy Shirley Pruitt's kayaking company—her dream since high school. Now she had to work for the new owner: Jaxon Pruitt, the bane of her existence.

But despite the unbridled hostility in her voice, he smiled at her in that half-lidded, ridiculously stomach-quivering way of his. "You didn't have the money to buy her out. I did."

"You don't have the experience to run the business." She ignored the fluttery feeling in her belly. "I do."

He shrugged. "We're at an impasse, then."

Jax was the poster boy for too-handsome-to-be-real. A perfect specimen of Uncle Sam's finest with his almost-grown-out military haircut.

He crossed his arms across his navy blue shirt. "How can we work this out?"

An outrageous combination of charm coupled with an aggravating self-confidence. And judging from the rippling muscles underneath his T-shirt, a hint of something slightly dangerous.

He opened his arms shoulder width. "I'm willing to do anything it takes to make this work." Shoulders that tapered to the narrow waist of his jeans.

She wrinkled her nose. "Frankly, Jaxon, I don't care what you—"

The bell clattered above the glass-fronted door, and Shirley burst inside. A little boy clung to her sturdy hand. She looked as if she'd been through a whirlwind.

Darcy found it hard to swallow past a sudden

lump in her throat. His mouth encircled by a ring of powdered sugar, the little guy was all Jax. Dark eyes, dark hair. So, so cute.

One day, he'd be handsome. As handsome as his dad. Jax would have to fight the girls off his son with a stick.

Jax crouched eye level to the child. "Looks like you enjoyed the Long Johns." He ruffled his son's hair.

But the small boy moved, putting himself out of reach of his father. Darcy's stomach knotted at the stark pain on Jax's face.

Shirley nudged the boy. "Tell your dad who we ran into at the Sandpiper."

The child inserted a thumb into his mouth. "No."

Hands on his thighs, Jax rocked onto his heels. "It's okay, Aunt Shirley. With my multiple deployments, Brody and I spent a lot of time apart. We're still getting reacquainted."

It wasn't okay. And from her taut expression, Shirley didn't think so, either.

"We ran into your mother, Darcy." Shirley laid her calloused hand on Brody's shoulder. "Agnes was quite taken with this little guy."

Darcy got on her knees in front of Brody. "Long Johns are my favorite, too."

Unmoving, the too-solemn child studied her.

Jax cleared his throat. "Son, I'd like you to meet my friend Darcy."

"Friend?" She and Anna had been BFFs. Him? Not so much.

A muscle ticked in his jaw. "We weren't enemies, were we?"

No, they hadn't been enemies.

Taking his thumb out of his mouth, Brody made a V with two fingers. "Me two." He uncurled another finger. "Thwee."

She turned to Jax for a translation.

"Brody will be three years old in September." He gave her a sheepish smile. "We're working on his *r*'s."

The child jabbed his thumb into his chest. "Me big."

"You are a big boy." She gave Brody an approving look. "A very big, strong boy."

He nodded, as somber as an undertaker. "Me Bwody Pwoo-it."

Darcy's heart turned over in her chest. "Hello, Brody Pruitt." She smiled at him.

Catching her by surprise, Brody touched a strand of her hair. "Pwetty."

She blushed. "Thank you, Brody."

Jax broadened his chest. "Good taste runs in his genes."

"Loves the ladies, does he?" She sneered at Jax. "Apples never fall far."

With his long legs extended and crossed at his booted ankles, Jax leaned his elbow on the counter. "I've always had a particular affection for trees."

Flushing, she shot to her feet so fast the room went cattywampus.

Instantly upright, Jax reached for her arm. "Darce?"

Anger—swift and hot—churned her gut. At his easy familiarity with her name. At...everything. She shook off his hand.

His face fell. "I didn't mean—"

"You never mean to do anything, do you, Jaxon?" She clenched her teeth.

"The two of you need to get it together." Shirley's forehead creased. "There's an excursion booked for Tuesday."

Darcy folded her arms. "I'm sure Jaxon can figure out whatever he needs to know."

His face pinched and sad, Brody stood knee-high between Shirley and Jax. And Darcy almost weakened. But Jaxon Pruitt and his son weren't her problem.

"I—I have to go." She rushed through the door as if her sanity depended on it. Where Jaxon Pruitt was concerned, it was not beyond the realm of possibility.

Stumbling outside, she stared at the gazebo on the village square. This couldn't be happening to her. There had to be some mistake.

But there was no mistake. Knuckle under to working with Jaxon Pruitt or find herself unemployed. Her choice.

Shirley stepped onto the porch. "Darcy... Please try to understand."

Darcy wheeled around. "You said whenever you decided to retire, you'd give me first dibs on buying the business."

She raised her eyebrow. "Did I say that?"

"You certainly led me to believe that. I believed we were friends."

Shirley had never fit into what most of her generation considered a proper role for a Southern woman. Instead of marriage and motherhood, she operated a successful water sports business. She was one of the first people to grasp the importance of ecotourism. She was also an environmental advocate in preserving the pristine beauty of the Delmarva Peninsula, bordered by the Atlantic on the east and the Chesapeake Bay on the west.

"We *are* friends, Darcy." Shirley's trim, athletic figure belied her sixty-plus years. "I need you to trust me when I tell you this arrangement is going to work out best for all of us."

Feeling the cool wind off the harbor, Darcy wrapped her bare arms around herself. "I'm sorry, but I don't see how any of this is in my best interest."

"Jaxon needs the shop more than you do."

This was so unfair. She'd spent years working her way to becoming Shirley's manager. She'd saved her money in preparation for one day assuming ownership.

"What about my ecotour certification? He doesn't have that." Darcy set her jaw. "Nor any experience in this business."

"He worked here in high school, like you."

Until Jax had graduated, joined the army and married overseas. She could feel pink breaching the collar of her cotton shirt. One of the downsides to being a strawberry blonde. Her every emotion was always on display.

But of all the people in the world, why did the new owner have to be him?

"Jaxon is struggling to readjust to civilian life, Darcy."

She threw out her hands. "So give him a job, Shirley. We hire extra people over the summer."

"Jaxon needs more than a part-time job. He needs a purpose. And a steady income to support his child. They need a home."

Darcy had a hard time envisioning Anna's foot-loose, marginally reckless, ever charming brother with a child. Or married. Except now he was a widower.

Her mouth thinned. "So you're saying this is my patriotic duty?"

"I'm only asking you to stay till summer's end. Help Jaxon learn the ropes."

Darcy shook her head. "He's your nephew. And I don't get your sudden need to retire."

"The timing of his return is a godsend." Shirley's eyes danced. "I've met someone."

Darcy blinked. "Who? When?"

"In January, during the winter kayaking season. He lives next door to my condo in the Keys." Shirley's no-nonsense face glowed. "He's retired Coast Guard. Like me, he loves to feel the sand between his toes."

This was so unlike the Shirley she'd always known, she was almost speechless. "Why haven't you said anything?"

Shirley shook her head. "You know how it is in Kiptohanock. Everybody in everybody else's business. I didn't want my family knowing until I was sure about the next step with Frank."

"But to leave everything? For a man you barely know?"

"Frank's a widower. His children and grandchildren are settled in Florida." Shirley sighed. "I'm willing to relocate for the sake of our relationship."

"Have you at least talked to my dad?"

"Your father, my pastor, gave me some good advice, which I intend to follow. It's time for a change in my life." Acquired after a lifetime of gauging sea horizons, Shirley's crow's-feet fanned into half-moons of joy.

In light of her obvious happiness, Darcy surrendered to the inevitable. "So what can I do to help?"

"Come winter, I'd like you to take over running the business in the Keys."

Her heart skipped a beat. She'd always longed

to travel. Now she'd get her chance. Though it would mean leaving everyone and everything she loved behind.

"But meanwhile…" Shirley took a deep breath. "Help me by helping my nephew find a place for himself here with his son."

Anything but that. Darcy squeezed her eyes shut. Thready panic fluttered like butterfly wings in her belly. "The Eastern Shore business for the Florida Keys branch?"

Shirley must've sensed her wavering resistance. "Please? You won't be sorry. I promise."

Darcy was already sorry. But as the daughter of the seaside hamlet's beloved Reverend Parks, she was nothing if not dutiful. The business would fail without her expertise. Jaxon would fail. Was she willing to stand by and watch that happen?

"If I agree…and that's a big if, Shirley," Darcy said, gritting her teeth. "I might consider helping once it gets busy, but when it comes to working with Jaxon on a daily basis, I can't make any promises."

"Just give it a try, and then come to Florida. If you decide that's what you truly want to do."

Darcy grimaced. "What else would I do? It's not like I have many options." Story of her life. And she was so sick of her life.

Not the only one who needed a change, maybe Shirley was right. Who wouldn't want to spend the winter in tropical Florida? Maybe this plan was best. Darcy just had to live through a summer of Jax.

Her heart sank.

When it came to Jaxon Pruitt, it was easier said than done.

Chapter Two

With more than a little reluctance, Darcy went inside the shop again with Shirley. Jax turned from the display kiosk. At his feet, Brody was stuffing a child-size Osprey backpack with everything within reach.

Jax tried taking hold of the pack. But scowling, his son hugged the lime-green bag to his chest.

"Brody likes to zip things," Jax murmured. "He was just playing. I'll put everything back where it belongs."

"It's your store. You can do what you want." She motioned to the backpack Brody clutched. "I like lime-green, too."

Jax shot her a glance. "I remember."

She ignored his overture. "Are you going on an expedition, Brody?"

Lips set in a thin line, Brody unzipped the bag. One by one, he removed the items he'd stashed, holding them up for her inspection. Cords, a pair of waterproof gloves, and carabiners. Which he clicked open and shut.

She smiled over his head to Jax. "Looks like you've got yourself a budding outdoorsman."

Uncoiling a notch, he gave her a tentative smile.

Shirley took hold of the little boy's hand. "You two should get to work. Since Brody's packed his gear, we'll take a stroll around the square. Take in the sights."

Darcy rolled her eyes. "That should take about five minutes." She helped Brody slip the pack on his back and tighten the straps.

"True." Shirley headed for the door. "But I also need more experience with little ones before I head to Florida this afternoon."

Darcy spent the next thirty minutes familiarizing Jax with shop merchandise and the online accounting system.

At a flicker of movement on the sandy beach outside, she looked up and saw Shirley giving Brody a beginner lesson on entering and exiting a kayak. The ecoentrepreneur didn't know much about children, but when in doubt, she fell back on what she did know. And Shirley knew kayaking.

Brody was too cute in his navy blue crocs, his legs straddling the child-sized kayak.

And with Jax engrossed in perusing the company website, she took her first good look at Brody's father. As lanky as ever, tall like all the Pruitt men. Corded muscles rippled along his forearms.

He'd fulfilled the physical potential of the boy she'd once known. Always handsome with his brown hair and melted-chocolate eyes. Problem was, back then he knew it. He knew just how to use his charm and good looks to his advantage.

The clean, pleasing aroma of his soap teased her nostrils. Her pulse jumped. She jolted at Jax's voice.

"How do you schedule the outings?"

The faster she updated Jaxon Pruitt on the business he'd bought out from under her, the faster she could return to her own life. Clicking the mouse, she showed him how to access the booking calendar.

"We offer one-to three-day kayaking expeditions, in addition to half-day trips. Anything from day-tripping to navigating the entire hundred-mile length of the Seaside Water Trail. From the tip of the peninsula at Cape Charles north to Chincoteague."

"Aunt Shirley did this by herself?"

Darcy shrugged. "After high school, I came on full-time. We worked in tandem on the water. But in the last few years, I've led the paddle groups while Shirley coordinated details at the shop."

Jax ticked through the website tabs. "Where do clients overnight on multiday expeditions?"

"For the more adventurous, we pitch tents on the barrier islands. Others prefer accommodations at B and Bs we've established relationships with, like the Duer Inn."

He rubbed the back of his neck.

"Of course, you'll need to teach paddle school before every excursion. And memorize the chart routes." At his dazed look, she stopped. "It's a lot to take in all at once."

His Adam's apple bobbed. "Yeah." His shoulders drooped.

At the uncertainty blanketing his features, a begrudging compassion filled her. "It will get easier, Jax."

His gaze cut to hers. "Will it?"

Darcy's breath hitched at his bleak expression. "Like riding a swell, it'll come back. You'll catch up." Her heart pounded. "I'll help."

"I need all the help I can get." His gaze shifted to the window. "Brody likes you." Jax's eyes dropped to the keyboard. "He's been so closed-off since his mother died. I'd begun to think he'd never—" His voice choked.

The Jax she remembered wasn't given to displays of emotion.

She closed the laptop. "Brody is a sweetheart. It's entirely my pleasure to know your son."

Giving Jax time to recover his self-control, she went over the list of gear presented to clients after booking an excursion.

He shuffled through a folder he'd brought with

him. "I've been thinking about a new marketing strategy to lure in more locals. What if we—"

"Not a good idea."

His nostrils flared. "How about listening before you dismiss my ideas?"

She jutted her chin. "How long has it been since you've been kayaking, Jax?"

His chiseled features hardened. "A while. Adrienne was from Utah. She preferred to snow ski."

"Well, here's a little news flash for you. Nothing—including kayaking—stood still while you were spanning the globe."

"I never said—"

"Typical Jaxon Pruitt. Always assuming he knows more than he really does."

He gritted his teeth. "That's not fair. Hear me out."

"Based on experience, I know locals aren't interested in the tours we operate. Nor, for the most part, able to pay the premium we charge."

"Darcy, I've been reading—"

"Reading?" She sniffed. "If only your high school English teacher had lived to see the day."

Jax exhaled. "Look, for this partnership to work we're both going to have to get on board with compromise. As the new owner, I think—"

"I wouldn't get on board with you, Jaxon Pruitt, if the ship was sinking and you were the last lifeboat available."

"Darcy, if you'd just—"

Scraping her chair across the tile, she rose. "We're done."

He got to his feet. "You'd rather drown than paddle with me?" His jaw went rock solid. "Fine."

Toe to toe with him, she glared. "Great."

His brows furrowed. "Fantastic."

She started for the door, her flip-flops punctuating her angry stride. "A jock like you shouldn't use big words he doesn't know how to spell."

"Takes one to know one."

She wheeled. "Did you call me a jock?"

Confusion flickered in his dark eyes. "Tomboy Darcy would've taken it as a compliment."

"Tomboys grow up." She curled her lip. "Something you should try."

"I didn't mean..." He growled. "Why do you have to be so obstinate, Darcy Parks? So hardheaded? So—"

She whirled toward the door. "Like you say, takes one to know one." Never looking back, she fluttered her hand over her shoulder. "Goodbye. Good riddance. Have yourself a good life, Jaxon Pruitt."

"Darce..."

Storming out, bell jangling, she let the slamming door frame her response.

Her and Jaxon Pruitt work together? Impossible. *He* was impossible. Same old arrogant jerk. She must've been delusional, imagining he'd acquired even a shred of humility.

She was breathing hard when she flung herself inside the SUV. Strangling the wheel, she forced herself to take a cleansing breath. Of all the people she'd ever known, Jaxon Pruitt possessed a rare ability to send her into orbit.

After cranking the key in the ignition, she pulled out of the parking lot and passed her father's car at the church. On Saturday afternoons, he liked to practice preaching his sermon to the empty sanctuary. Reverend Parks would've told her she needed to pray about her attitude. Like Jax didn't?

When she rounded the village green, one of the volunteer firefighters waved from the open bay of the station. Small town friendliness. Some things never changed. Which used to drive her crazy. But now?

There was something incredibly soothing and comforting about the unchanging rhythm of life on the Eastern Shore. As predictable as the tide. A surety in an otherwise uncertain world that, at age thirty, she'd finally learned to appreciate.

A cocoon of safety... She grimaced. Until Jaxon and his heart-stealing son had arrived.

Completing her drive-by of the square, she turned into one of the residential side streets radiating out from the green like the spokes of a wheel.

Oaks and maples arched over the street. Streaming through the foliage, sunshine splattered the sidewalk. Averting her gaze from Jaxon's family home, she pulled into the driveway of the neighboring Victorian parsonage, her home since birth.

Such a cliché. Literally, the girl next door. After parking in the half-circle drive, she trudged toward the backyard, where Shore folk did most of their living. She was careful to keep her eyes averted from the towering tree between the Parks and Pruitt yards as she plodded up the concrete steps to the screened porch.

Darcy let the door slam behind her. It was that kind of day. "Mom?"

"In here."

Stepping out of her flip-flops, she ventured inside the house. Her mother straightened from the oven, a casserole dish cradled in her mitted hands. Coils of steam rose from the lasagna. Mouthwatering aromas permeated the kitchen.

Agnes smiled. "I made the lasagna this morning. After talking with Shirley at the Sandpiper, I only had to reheat the pan."

Darcy glanced at the kitchen clock. "Kind of early for dinner."

Her mother placed the hot dish in a padded, insulated carrier. "Not by the time you take this out to Shirley's house for Jaxon."

"Oh, no, I'm not."

Agnes cocked her head. "Shirley left those boys with only milk in the fridge and cereal in the pantry."

Hands raised, Darcy stepped back. "One of those boys is a combat veteran. He can fend for himself."

"But Jaxon always loved my lasagna."

Darcy gave her a brittle smile. "Since nobody's seen him in fourteen years, maybe it's the only thing hc loved about his hometown."

Her mom's denim-blue eyes softened.

Darcy stiffened. She knew the look. The kill-her-with-kindness approach. She must not weaken. She must not...

"I don't think that's true, Darcy." Her mother shifted to her I'm-so-disappointed-in-you look. "And what's more, I don't think you believe that, either."

"Jax can buy his own groceries. He can fix his own dinner. He doesn't need our help."

"I wouldn't be so sure about that." Agnes's mouth quirked. "Jaxon will have his hands full getting settled into his new home tonight. Think of his son."

Adorable Brody Pruitt was the last person she wanted to think about. No, that wasn't true. Brody's father was the last person she wanted to think about.

Her mother gestured next door. "With his parents out of town, they probably haven't had a decent meal yet."

"Jax looked just fine to me."

"Did he now?" Her mother's eyes twinkled.

"That's not what I meant and you know it." Darcy bit her lip.

Agnes placed a container of pimento cheese into a wicker basket. "They're both too skinny. Especially Brody. He's a growing boy. He needs to eat."

Darcy folded her arms. "Why don't *you* take it to them?"

"Your father would want to make sure Jaxon and his little orphan son were properly welcomed home…"

It was all Darcy could do not to roll her eyes at the word *orphan*. But being the dutiful daughter she'd always been, she didn't. PKs—preacher's kids—never behaved disrespectfully.

Then her beloved mother played her last, most effective card.

"I guess when your dad returns…" Agnes placed a bunch of bananas in the basket. "Although your father usually tries to rest before his busiest day of the week. But we could drop everything… Head out there…" She emitted a long-drawn-out sigh.

Darcy thrust out her hand. "Just give me the basket, Mom. I'll take it out there, already."

Her mother beamed. "How nice of you to offer."

Darcy snorted. Not only unladylike, but also very unPK.

Her mother's unique blend of strong-armed gentleness would have made her a superb peace negotiator. But perhaps as a pastor's wife, that's exactly what she was—navigating the not-always-serene waters of Kiptohanock life.

Agnes removed a pie from the refrigerator. "Shirley tells me you still need to brief Jaxon on the map route for the upcoming excursion."

"How did you—?" Darcy glanced at the old-fashioned landline phone hanging on the wall. "You and Shirley were pretty sure of yourselves, weren't you, Mom?"

"By now, Shirl's probably on her way to the toll plaza at the bridge." Agnes smoothed her apron. "Don't be angry. I felt confident you'd do the right thing. As you always do."

That was her. Boring, dutiful Darcy. PK extraordinaire.

Her mother plucked a loaf of bread off the countertop. "Besides, don't you think it's time you confronted this thing between you and Jaxon?"

Mouth gaping, eyes wide—with horror—Darcy drew up. "There isn't a thing between Jax and me."

Her mom arched her eyebrow. "Then what's the big deal in helping him for a few months?"

Darcy's heart raced. "The big deal is…" She threw out her hands. "No one seems to understand that I'm the wronged one here."

Her mother's gaze sharpened. "Tell me the truth. Why are you so afraid of helping Jaxon?"

Darcy sucked in a breath. "I'm not afraid of him."

"No, my dear brave girl." Her mother touched her arm. "You're afraid of yourself."

She jerked free. "That's not true."

"I think your father and I made the nest too cozy. But that's no way to live, honey. It's time to venture out. Test your wings and fly." She placed her palm against Darcy's cheek. "Don't lock your heart away from the possibility of a new life."

Was her mom right? Was she afraid to reach for more? "Shirley told you about me moving to Florida?"

Agnes fiddled with a tray of deli meat and sandwich rolls.

Darcy blinked. "How long have you and Shirley been planning this ambush, Mom?"

"Shirley came to us with the decision to sell the business to Jaxon." Her mother gave Darcy a small smile. "A decision with which your father and I agreed. We see a lot of Shirley in you."

"And what's wrong with that?" Darcy narrowed her eyes. "Shirley has built a successful business."

"There's nothing wrong with being independent. But at this point in her life, her choices have left her lonely. Your father and I, we want more for you."

"Dad is in on this, too?"

"Your father wants to see you happy." Moisture filled Agnes's eyes. "God—via Shirley—has given you another opportunity."

"So you'd both be okay if I move to Florida?"

Her mother gave a slow nod. "If Florida will make you truly happy."

Almost Shirley's exact words.

"Did moving to the parsonage make you truly happy, Mom?"

Agnes gripped the basket handle. "It did." But her mouth tightened.

They were Harold Parks's second family. Thirty-five years ago, his first wife and son had tragically died in a car accident. Something Darcy's father never spoke about. Her mother, either.

His replacement wife. His runner-up family. Like Darcy with the Florida business. And she was tired of feeling like the runner-up, the consolation prize.

Did her mother know that every August 14 her father visited the tiny cemetery outside town?

"I'm not like you, Mom. Not everyone wants to be a wife and mother." She lifted her chin. "I'd never be happy at the beck and call of the entire village."

Her mother straightened. "Maybe not. But pursuing your dreams doesn't have to exclude loving relationships." Her forehead puckered. "Don't waste this chance or this summer, Darcy. For your own sake, sweetheart. Please."

"Your kind of happiness won't work for me."

"But Darcy, suppose this summer is about more than kayaking?"

"I don't know what you mean."

Her mother flipped the basket lid shut. "Life is a journey. Like love. And you never know what might lie beyond the next bend."

Darcy huffed. "Better paddle harder. I think I hear banjos."

Her mother—pastor's wife, former social worker and everyone's favorite friend—crinkled her eyes at Darcy. "If nothing else, be kind to a lonely little boy who's lost his mother and everything he ever knew."

Bull's eye. The chink in Darcy's armor. Despite being an only child—maybe because of being a lonely only—she loved children.

And so fifteen minutes later, she stowed the basket in the SUV. Her mother waved from the front lawn.

Darcy told herself she was doing this only for Brody. She couldn't get the image of his sad face out of her mind, and thoughts of the withdrawn little guy lay heavy on her heart. Getting an idea, she made a quick detour north on Highway 13 to the dollar store.

The vibe between Jax and his son continued to gnaw at her. Back in the car, she ventured off the main road toward Shirley's wooded farmhouse, situated on an isolated neck of the inlet.

Was her mom right? Was this summer about more than merely keeping a business afloat? Turning off Seaside Road, the SUV bounced across the rutted drive.

On the football field, Jax had possessed a daring recklessness. Like each of the overachieving Pruitts—Ben the Annapolis grad, Will the firefighter, dad and brother Charlie deputy sheriffs—fear had never been a factor for Green Beret Jax.

But now? A memory arose in her mind of an incident that had happened a few years ago, after the hurricane tore through Kiptohanock.

A golden retriever had floundered in the harbor off the jetty. In the dog's eyes she'd beheld the same expression she'd glimpsed in Jax's face this afternoon when he gazed at his son. Despair and an overwhelming fear.

Steering the SUV through the grove of trees, she winced at the memory of that day. Losing strength, the retriever had appeared about to go under. Just like Jaxon Pruitt?

Disturbed by the comparison, she gripped the wheel. She'd dived into the churning water without hesitation to rescue the dog. And kept the retriever afloat long enough for a Coastie to jump in and get them both to safety. Later, the owners had gratefully reclaimed their pet.

Was that what God wanted her to do with Jax and Brody? Get them to a safe place? Was this summer about keeping them afloat until they gained a foothold of trust with each other? At stake was Brody's relationship with his dad.

As to her own continuing proximity with Brody's widowed father? Darcy released a slow trickle of breath. This wouldn't end well.

Because where Jaxon Pruitt was concerned, it never had. Not for her.

Chapter Three

Jaxon tucked Brody's folded shirts and jeans into the bureau drawer. The socks and Spider-Man underwear went into another drawer. Hand on his hips, Jax glanced around the bedroom.

He'd purchased the rambling, three-bedroom farmhouse from his aunt as part of their business deal. At present, the house was furnished with only the bare essentials. As spartan and unsentimental as his aunt, it would be up to Jax to figure out how to turn the house into a home for Brody.

What Jax knew about kids—despite being the oldest of four brothers and one sister—wouldn't fill Brody's pint-size suitcase.

Stowing the suitcase in the hall closet, he headed down the creaking staircase to check on his son. And found him where he'd left him ten minutes ago. Knees planted in the sofa cushion, Brody kept his eyes fastened on the winding driveway. As if he was waiting for someone.

Watching for someone—like his mother?—who'd never return.

Guilt twisted Jax's gut. "What're you doing, son?"

Brody didn't turn around. "Hungwy."

Him, too. "Let's get chicken nuggets at McDonald's."

Brody shook his head, but his fixation on the driveway didn't waver. "No 'Donalds."

Jax was also tired of fast food. It had been a long day, starting with the drive over the Bay Bridge Tunnel. With the waves lapping the shoreline in Virginia Beach, they'd crossed the steel-girded artery which connected what been here, born heres called the Western Shore of mainland Virginia to their Eastern Shore home.

Brody probably should've had a nap. But perched high in his car seat, he'd studied the shorebirds wheeling overhead, the silent child as emotionally remote as Jax himself.

Apples and trees. Fathers and sons. He scrubbed his hand over his face. Bringing up the tree thing with Darcy had been a mistake. A tactical error in winning her support.

He needed her help or this attempt at a new life was doomed. But he'd gone too fast, pushing his business ideas on her. Neither of them were the same carefree kids they'd been. And now he'd blown any hope of friendship, much less a business collaboration.

And there remained his biggest dilemma—how to reach his son. As he knelt there staring through the window, Brody's skinny shoulder blades stood out through his Power Rangers T-shirt.

"What 'bout cereal, Brode?"

Home less than a day, Jax had already slipped into his native speech. *Bogue, fogue* and *dogue* were sure to follow for bog, fog and dog.

"No…" An unaccustomed whine had crept into Brody's too stoic voice.

Better forget Brody's usual tub time. Jax wasn't sure he had the fortitude to gator wrestle a two-year-old, slippery as an eel, into a bath. He'd feed Brody and put him to bed.

As for the upcoming kayaking excursion? He rolled his neck and shoulders, trying to work out the kinks. He also needed to study the water charts for the Tuesday morning expedition.

"How 'bout pizza, son?"

An SUV rounded the curve in the driveway. Darcy's SUV. Jax's heartbeat accelerated. Brody launched himself off the couch and grabbed the doorknob.

Jax scrambled after him. "Wait, Brody." But somehow the child managed to pry open the door. Who knew a two-year-old could be so fast?

As Jax stepped onto the wraparound porch, his son hurled himself at Darcy. His arms clasped around her legs, Brody buried his face in her jeans. "Me know you come, Dawcy. Me know."

Darcy's eyes went wide. Jax stood frozen. A wicker basket lay in the gravel beside her. A plastic shopping bag dangled from her hand.

Brody had been waiting and watching for Darcy? After what happened earlier, Jax had feared they'd seen the last of her. Yet here she was. And with a childlike faith, Brody had believed she'd come.

Jax moved to ground level. "Let me take something." He grabbed hold of the basket.

"Thanks."

His arms sagged at the basket's weight. "Wow, how did you get this thing out of the car?"

"When will you learn, Pruitt, it's all about girl power?"

She'd been telling him that since she was only slightly older than Brody. His mouth curved. "How could I forget?"

With her free hand, she cupped Brody's head. But her gaze never left Jax. "See that you don't, Pruitt."

She drew back, though, when he reached for the plastic bag. "It's a surprise for later."

Letting go of her legs, Brody turned his face up to her. "'Pwize?"

She pointed to the hamper. "Only if you eat a good dinner."

Brody's stomach rumbled, and he laughed.

Jax almost dropped the basket. "That's the first

time I've heard him laugh since..." Chest heaving, he gulped past the boulder lodged in his throat.

Darcy's lips quivered. "I'm glad."

He was glad she was here. But he couldn't say that to her. That had never been the way they were with each other. Instead, he took a lungful of the scents wafting from the basket. "Something smells great."

She shrugged. "Mom was convinced you two would die of starvation without a home-cooked meal tonight."

He'd always loved her mother, Agnes, a quiet, sweet spirit more comfortable behind the scenes than center stage. With his own mother off-Shore right now, somehow she'd known what he and Brody needed most was a taste of home.

"Lasagna. Half spinach for Brody, meat for a carnivore like you." Darcy squared her shoulders. "Also included, lunch fixings for tomorrow. And a pie tonight if both of you are very good boys."

"Me wuv pie." Propped against her thigh, Brody sighed, a sound of utter contentment.

Not unlike what Jax was feeling. Suddenly, the world seemed a better place. Despite the fading sunlight, a happier, brighter place.

She bit her lip. "Would Brody let me pick him up, Jax?"

"Not me, but you he might."

Flushing, he dropped his eyes at the painful admission. She must think him a terrible father. His own son didn't want Jax to hold him.

She opened her arms, and Brody didn't hesitate. He leaped into her embrace. Jax pushed aside a sting of envy.

He heaved the basket up the steps. "I'll call your mom later and thank her."

At the door, he paused, keeping his back to Darcy. "Seems like a ton of food for just the little guy and me. Would you stay and help us?"

He was asking for more than dinner. They both knew it. And if she refused? He wasn't sure how he'd cope with another rejection from her today.

The silence stretched. He closed his eyes, but didn't turn around. His heart pounded in his ears.

"I'll stay."

Opening his eyes, he released a breath.

She lugged his son, propped on her hip, onto the porch. "After dinner, I'll go over the map route with you."

He held the door for her. "I'd appreciate it."

In the kitchen, he set out the food on the butcher-block countertop. He hadn't had time to explore the kitchen, but he needn't have worried. She immediately pulled out plates and removed glasses from the cabinet next to the sink.

"You've spent a lot of time here with Shirley."

Darcy opened a utensil drawer. "She mentored me."

And therefore, Darcy was far much more deserving of this opportunity than him. No wonder she resented him. No wonder she didn't want to work with him.

Darcy showed Brody how to fold the paper napkins, and his little man toddled around the farmhouse table, setting out three places.

She knew the kayaking business, and Jax didn't. It should be her name on the company title, not his. If it weren't for Brody, he'd...

Jax dug into the casserole. For Brody's sake, what choice did he have? The papers were signed. The deal was done.

And he was so profoundly grateful for this chance to come home. To have a job. A purpose and a way to provide a life for his son.

Jax spooned out the lasagna onto the plates. Darcy rigged a stack of phone books onto one of the chairs as a booster seat.

He poured milk for Brody into a small juice cup. "I'm surprised anyone uses telephone books anymore."

She lifted Brody to the top of the stack. "Shirley is old-school."

Jax cut the spinach lasagna into bite-size pieces for Brody. "So it was you behind the website."

She held up a salad fork. "Can Brody use this?"

Jax grinned over his son's dark head. "Let's just say he gives it a good try."

She smiled at him. A lot of firsts tonight. His pulse ratcheted.

Darcy tucked a napkin in the neck of Brody's shirt. "He'll get the hang of it. Like you with this single parenting thing."

"I appreciate your confidence in me."

She arched her eyebrow. "Confidence has never been a problem for Jaxon Pruitt."

Gripping the fork, Brody speared a noodle.

"Uh, wait a minute, Brody." She placed a restraining hand on his arm. "We need to tell God thanks for the food."

Something else Jax had failed to do as a parent. His stomach tightened. But she flicked a quick smile at him.

"Put down the fork, Brody, and put your hands together like this. Close your eyes."

His little hands folded underneath his chin. "Like Gwandma."

Jax nodded. "Like Grandma."

When his parents came to help with Brody's care in the months following Adrienne's death, his mother had taught Brody to pray. A good practice Jax had allowed to lapse. A good habit he needed to reinstate.

Brody squeezed his eyes shut. "'Kay, Dawcy."

A smile hovering on her lips, she closed her eyes, too. "Dear Father, thank You for this day and for the food."

Not closing his eyes, Jax studied Darcy's face, as usual bare of anything beyond sunscreen. Her sweeping lashes lay soft against her cheeks.

"Thank You for the hands that prepared this wonderful food. Thank You for Brody."

His son's mouth tipped up at the corners.

She lifted her face toward the ceiling, like a sunflower seeking light. "Thank You for Brody's daddy."

Jax stilled.

She opened her eyes and looked at him. "And thank You for bringing Brody and his dad home to Kiptohanock."

"Amen," Jax whispered.

She cleared her throat. "Amen, Brody. Now you can eat."

Brody's eyes flew open. "Ay-ay-men…"

They laughed.

Keeping an eye on Brody's attempt to lance the lasagna and access his mouth, Jax sat across from Darcy. "The confident Jaxon Pruitt you remember didn't quite make it back from an Afghan province."

She handed him a plate of lasagna. "What about the commendations under fire? Jax the Invincible."

"Not so invincible." He paused, fork midway to his mouth. "You kept track of me?"

She stabbed the lasagna on her plate. "Not so hard with the Kiptohanock grapevine at work. You know how it is in a small town."

"Home sweet home," he grunted. "Where *you*

may not know what you're doing, but you can rest assured everyone else does."

"Ain't that the truth." She rolled her eyes. "But in your case, you've always succeeded at everything you attempted."

"In hindsight, too easily. Without having to try too hard." He bent over the plate. "And when it really matters, like now…"

She laid down her fork. "You are a naturally gifted athlete. Easy on the eyes. And despite the laid-back demeanor, intelligent. You'll be an old hand at running the kayaking business before you know it."

His head came up. "You think I'm good-looking?"

Darcy's mouth opened and closed like a fish on a hook. "That's what you got out of everything I said? Good-looking cannot be a news flash to you."

He cocked his head. "The news flash is that you think so, too."

"All the Pruitt men are good-looking." She gave him a sideways glance. "Though your baby brother, Charlie, is widely considered the most handsome of the bunch. Not you."

He placed his hand over his chest. "Zing— straight through the heart." He laughed. "I missed you, Darcy."

She could always be counted on to give him a

healthy dose of humility. Whether he wanted her to or not.

"Did you? I couldn't tell."

Brody reached for his cup, and she jumped up—as did Jax—a second too late to prevent a milk mishap.

Jax righted the overturned cup. "I'm sorry about what happened this afternoon. You're right. I need to learn the business before I make changes."

She used her napkin to mop up the spill. "I should've given your ideas a chance. Maybe next week—things are slow until summer cranks up— we could revisit your idea. It's your business. You're the boss."

"Next week? Does that mean you'd be willing to teach me what you know?"

"Providing we can come to acceptable terms."

Darcy took life on her terms. One of the things he'd most liked about her when they were children. Because truth be told, he was the same way. Frenemies or not, they'd always understood each other.

At least until that last summer before he shipped out to Basic. Things had gotten confusing between them.

He pushed back his shoulders. "Okay, hit me."

"Don't tempt me." She ran her finger around the rim of her glass. "When will you learn not to say things you don't mean?"

He laughed. In the old days, she'd always managed to make him laugh. Most of all, at himself. "I meant hit me with your terms."

She leaned forward, elbows on the table. "I'll teach you what I know about the business, but after Labor Day I'm leaving the Shore to run Shirley's operation in the Keys. You'll have three months to get up to speed, but after that you're on your own."

Just when he returned, she was leaving? The sunshine girl headed to the Sunshine State. But she'd offered him an olive branch. A truce in their long-running battle of hostility.

"You were gone a long time." She settled into her chair. "Why didn't you ever come back?"

"I was nineteen the first time I deployed, Darcy." He took a deep breath. "Somewhere along the way, I got lost."

"Lost how?"

His shoulders rose and fell. "Let's just say I've been as far from Kiptohanock as you can find yourself and still be on the same planet." He looked away. "These last few days since leaving Salt Lake City, I've asked myself if it was possible to fit into small town life again. But for Brody's sake..."

She placed her palms flat on either side of her plate. "It's because of Brody that I know you're going to make this work, Jax."

He frowned. "You've got more faith in me than I do in myself right now."

"You are the king of don't quit, Jaxon Pruitt." She smirked. "Obnoxiously so. You'll rise to the occasion. You always do."

"Somewhere in there I think there was a compliment." He ran his fingers through the short ends of his hair. "A very hidden compliment."

Darcy tilted her head. "And here's something else I've learned about small towns like Kiptohanock."

He took a swig of sweet tea, as much as anything to give his hands something to do. "What's that?"

"Sometimes small towns are so out in the middle of nowhere that you have to get lost to find them."

He gnawed at his lower lip. "You're saying even lost, I'm right where I should be?"

"Small town life lesson." She gave him a lopsided smile. "I won't charge you for that one. But I'll expect to receive my paycheck as usual at the end of the month."

"Duly noted." He rested against the chair. "I never realized until I left how much I'd miss this place."

"For born heres—" she placed her hand over her heart "—it becomes a part of us."

"I took being within sight and sound of the water for granted. It's who we are in the deep places. Over there I lost the best part of myself."

He fiddled with his silverware. "But if you don't mind me asking—"

"Like that's ever stopped you before."

"Why are you leaving, Darcy?"

"The longer I've stayed—maybe I've over-stayed—the more lost I feel." She averted her eyes. "Perhaps it's time for me to see if there's more out there."

"Does more have to be out there? Not here?"

Her gaze returned to his. "I thought you'd understand, Jax. We're both all-or-nothing people."

"You want to know the real reason I didn't return until now?" His heart drummed in his chest. "I didn't think there could ever be a place here for me again."

"But you're home now, Jax."

"Am I?" He studied her. "Will you forgive me, Darcy?"

His question was about so much more than what had happened this afternoon.

She looked at him. "I'm here, aren't I?"

"Can we get back to being friends?" He thrust out his chin. "We were friends, Darcy. Once."

"Trust might be trickier than merely coming home."

Jax tightened his jaw. "A chance is all I'm asking."

His son pushed off from the table. "Pie?"

Bolting to his feet, Jax grabbed for the sliding phone books.

She caught his son underneath his arms. "Whoa, there, Brody Pruitt. What's the rush?"

His mouth and chin were covered in red sauce. "Me Bwody Pwoo-it, Dawcy." He raised his sauce-encrusted hands.

She kissed a clean spot on the top of his head. "Yes, you are. And what you are is a big mess."

Brody threw back his head and belly-laughed.

"You know, Jaxon Pruitt, you have an irresistible son."

He polished his knuckles on his shirt. "Like father, like son."

"You wish."

Smiling, he cut Brody a sliver of pie while Darcy made a valiant attempt to restore a semblance of cleanliness to his son.

After dessert, she took out a small plastic bottle from the shopping bag. "Bubbles, Brody. Let's go out back."

She guided him down the deck stairs to the tree-studded, sloping lawn. The meandering tidal creek glistened like multicolored jewels in the rainbow hue of the fiery sunset.

Darcy handed Jax a large bubble wand. "This one's for you."

Brody quivered with excitement. She dabbed the tiny stick in the solution. And pursing her lips, she blew across the wand.

A single bubble hung suspended before a soft breeze off the salt marsh lifted it into the air. They watched as the bubble rose higher and higher until it disappeared over the trees.

"Oh, Dawcy..." For the first time since Adrienne's death, Brody smiled.

Darcy's eyes welled and cut to Jax. His eyelids burned. She understood what this moment meant.

"Thank you, Darce."

As soon as he said the old nickname, he remembered how she hated it. Yet old habits died hard. Like old loves?

But this time, a smile flitted across her lips. "You're welcome, Jax."

His son bounced, a human pogo stick. "Mow, Dawcy. Mow."

"Surc thing." She blew another bubble.

Brody's arms reached above his hcad.

She motioned. "Go get it, Brody."

He raced aftcr the bubble. Buoyant on the wind, it eluded his grasp. She blew bubble after bubble as Brody gave chase. His son laughed and laughed. As if making up for lost time.

Happiness. Peace. Contentment. Always just out of Jax's grasp, too. Eluding him all these years.

"Watch this, Brody," she called.

Brody wheeled.

She nudged Jax. "Bend a little and close your eyes."

He obliged, and she leaned closer. Close enough for him to feel her breath on his face as she blew gently across the small wand.

A bubble tickled his eyelids and danced like a frolicking ladybug across his skin. A caress. A whisper. A promise?

Brody clapped his hands. "Me, Dawcy. Me."

"You can open your eyes, Jax."

So he did. Her own eyes hooded, she touched her finger to the cleft in his chin. Just for a second before she moved to his son.

Brody chuckled when the bubbles brushed his shuttered eyelids. "Me do you, Dawcy."

Keeping hold of the bottle, she let Brody dip the stick into the liquid.

"Cwoser, Dawcy. Cwoser."

Jax rubbed his forehead. "He has trouble with *l*'s, too."

Crouching to Brody's height, she clamped her eyes shut. And flinched when what she got from him was more spit than bubble.

"Way to take one for the team, Darce."

She shoulder-butted him. "Your turn, soldier."

"At your peril, Darcy Parks." He stepped back, yanking the large bubble wand from its sheath.

"Ooh…" Brody's eyes rounded.

Brandishing it like a saber, Jax smiled, slashing the air between them. She smiled back at him.

And he knew she remembered childhood escapades involving pretend pirates in the tree house. Zorro and intergalactic warfare, too. They'd made it up as they went along. Like now?

He whirled, loosing a giant bubble blob. Brody cackled with sheer delight.

Darcy ran toward the creek. "Catch it, Brody!"

The toddler raced after her as fast as his small legs allowed. He stumbled, but she was there, sweeping him into her arms.

Jax's heart caught in his throat.

For the first time, he thought he might've found a way to bridge the gap. The answer to a prayer he'd been too afraid to voice. Could it be that with Darcy's help, he might've found the way home for both of them?

Chapter Four

On Mondays, the shop was closed. A well-earned rest for employees who spent the weekend guiding kayaking tours. Usually Darcy slept in on her day off. Mondays—not Sundays, though she'd never tell her minister father—were her favorite day of the week.

She hadn't seen Jax since Saturday night, nor did he appear at church. But Monday morning, despite sleeping fitfully, she came fully awake at 6:00 a.m. Wired, restless, vaguely uneasy.

Darcy lay in bed, watching the first beams of light filter through the dormer window. She'd lived in this house as long as she'd been alive.

Mondays were also her father's well-earned day off. The day he chose her and her mom over the rest of his congregation. In the summers when she was out of school, they'd spent the day as a family doing fun stuff.

During the school year, she still remembered

the special thrill of getting off the bus at the square and walking the last few blocks home with the Pruitt clan.

Her steps quick with anticipation, she knew her father would be waiting for her at the base of the tree house. He'd push her on the swing, and they'd spend a blissful hour together. She loved to swing, trying to touch the sky.

"I'm a swing kind of girl!" she'd call, pumping her legs as hard as she could go.

"And I'm a swing kind of dad," her father would say back.

On the swing, she could fly. Feeling free and light, she broke the bonds of gravity and soared into the wild blue yonder.

Being so energetic, she must've wearied her more sedentary parents. No wonder they were content for her to play with the Pruitt pack next door.

A Kiptohanock native, her father had become pastor of the church with a wife and a young son in tow. The wife and son Darcy never knew. Because if they'd lived, Harold Parks would never have married her mother, and Darcy Parks wouldn't exist.

She gazed at the ceiling. It was strange to think of herself as not existing. And equally strange to contemplate why she lived and yet her father's other child had not.

Over the years, she'd thought a lot about her

brother. Would she and Colin have been friends, like the Pruitt siblings? Perhaps the two of them would've gone fishing. Hunted for seashells on one of the barrier islands.

Would he have been bookish like their father? Or athletic like her, who took after nobody on either side of the family? Truth was, dead little Colin Parks had fit in better with her father than she ever would.

She flung back the thin sheet and swung her legs over the side of the bed. Enough of that. Not given to melancholy, her perennially cheerful mother had raised her to be the same. Darcy was far more comfortable with doing something rather than just being.

Careful to avoid the pine floorboard that creaked, she quietly dressed lest she awaken her parents. Sunday was her dad's busiest day, and on Mondays he needed his rest. He continued to maintain the pastoral duties of a much younger man.

Standing at the kitchen sink eating a banana, she watched the sun rise over the treetops. No lights shone from the Pruitt house, but Everett Pruitt's charcoal-gray SUV sat in the driveway. Jax's parents must've arrived home last night.

Brody was too little for kayaking. Jax would need his parents' help with Brody when he was working.

The Pruitts had always been great neighbors.

Darcy loved Jax's mother. Gail Pruitt, a busy RN with five rambunctious children of her own, always made room at the table for one more—the lonely only PK.

Darcy drifted onto the screened porch, stuffing her bare feet into the flip-flops she'd left there last night. Easing the screen door shut behind her, she plodded toward the tree house.

Underneath the massive oak, the swing moved idly in the desultory breeze blowing in from the harbor. Hand on the railing, she climbed past the lower platform. The wooden steps wound around the tree trunk, and she ascended to her favorite spot on the higher second level. Rising out of the tree canopy, the perch provided a bird's-eye view of the entire village.

She settled into one of the lawn chairs she kept there. Not that anyone but her had been here for a long time. The Pruitts had outgrown the tree house. Just as, one by one, they'd each outgrown the need for home. And her.

How pathetic was it that she still came up here? Almost thirty, she still lived at home. No boyfriend—or prospects for one—and no real life of her own. What did she have to show for the last fourteen years of her life?

Yet every morning she climbed the tree house stairs. Here, God felt very near. Almost near enough to touch. Almost as close as the clouds overhead. And at night, this was the perfect spot to view God's starry handiwork.

She'd spent hours here as a child. Vicariously enjoying the noise, laughter and life emanating from the house next door. But she'd been too shy to venture over, until the day Jax stood at the bottom of the tree and invited her to come play with his little sister.

"Anna's always bothering me and Ben," Jax had called up. "You'd be doing us a favor."

Coaxed out, she'd kept a wary eye on the oldest Pruitt boy as she climbed down from the branches. Even from a distance, she knew him to be a charming handful to his mother and his Sunday-school teachers.

On that sultry summer day she never forgot, the Pruitt kids had smiled at her, their mouths stained purple, red, orange and blue.

Jax had handed her a slushy freezer pop. "You look like lime-green would be your favorite."

Oh so grateful to be included, she took it from him. Thereafter, when the Pruitts broke out freezer pops, the lime-green was forever hers.

Darcy closed her eyes, remembering. The breeze rustled the leaves of the tree. If only she could recapture those days. Before she'd known about the other family. When she felt loved and chosen, blissfully unaware of her father's heartache.

Things between her and Jax had changed his senior year in high school. Under the basketball net at the end of the Pruitt driveway, he'd gotten all over Will, who'd accidentally knocked her down. Jax had never cared before if anyone wiped the concrete with her.

At youth group, he'd looked at her differently. He would flush when she caught him staring. Drop his eyes. Scuff the toe of his sneaker in the dirt. Awkward, un-Jax-like.

Then after dinner that spring, he took to climbing into the tree house. They'd sit in silence—again, very un-Jax-like. Watching the fireflies blink around them. Watching the stars wink overhead.

Small talk at first. Had she seen the game on TV? What did she think about their chances for beating the church league team in nearby Onley next week? Gradually, he'd told her how he wanted to serve his country like his grandfather. How he wanted to see the world and live life without reservations, on the edge.

He'd painted an irresistible picture of adventure. The kind of adventure she secretly longed for. Living life to the fullest, though part of her shied away from the prospect of leaving everyone and everything behind. Her ideal life would be a balance of the two—home and adventure.

She'd believed Jax Pruitt was the bravest boy she'd ever known. The most handsome. The most everything.

A late bloomer, Darcy found that boys didn't give her much attention. They respected her athletic ability. Admired her tough, never-say-die spirit. But when it came time for the prom, she wasn't the girl they asked.

She was flattered, frankly, that Jax Pruitt spent so many of his evenings in the treetop with her. They never held hands or anything like that. He never touched her. They never kissed. Skittish as she was, she would've probably decked him if he'd tried. Not that he would've tried anything. She was the PK, after all.

But things between them definitely altered. Beyond the tree house, they'd spent an enormous amount of time together working at his aunt Shirley's shop that summer. And Darcy had loved every minute of it.

As a very sheltered, immature sixteen-year-old, she'd had feelings she didn't know what to do with. She'd dreaded the day Jax would report to Basic at summer's end.

Knowing something was coming didn't always make it better. Like watching a hurricane offshore creep ever closer. Understanding the devastation the day would bring and yet unable to stop it from happening.

"Wait for me in the tree," Jax had told her in his husky voice. The voice he used with her. "I'll be there first thing in the morning to say goodbye." He'd also promised to write.

She didn't sleep that night. She got up early to wait for him in the tree house. He never showed.

The house next door lay strangely quiet. The Pruitt car had already gone from the driveway. And Jax Pruitt never wrote her. Not once. The old ache resurfaced.

Returning to the present, Darcy exhaled. Ironic that Jax's return to Kiptohanock meant that, ready or not, her own adventures were about to begin. It was probably good she didn't have to see Jax or his beguiling son today. Monday couldn't have been more perfectly timed.

"Darcy?" Her mother stood on the bottom step, peering through the branches. "What in the world are you doing up there so early, sweetie?"

She sighed. "Thinking."

Praying. Trying to gather the courage to reach for a life full of the adventures she'd once dreamed about. But she didn't say that to her mom. She couldn't. PKs didn't do that sort of thing, after all.

"Your father said something about going to Assateague today. You want to join us?"

Assateague meant the beach, climbing the red-brick lighthouse again, and at the Island Creamery, eating the best ice cream on the peninsula. "Coming."

She hurried down the stairs. A perfect day spent with those she loved most. She loved Mondays.

Pulling into the driveway, Jax immediately glanced next door. Darcy's SUV was parked there, but her father's compact car was missing. No signs of life at the bungalow.

But it was Monday, of course. Darcy's favorite day. His lips curved, and his gaze skirted to the backyard oak, its branches visible above the roof of the house.

"Gwandma?" Brody piped from his car seat.

Jax's mother stepped onto the porch and waved. He'd spent the day fleshing out his ideas for expanding the business, while Brody sat in front of the television set.

He unhooked Brody's harness. Not good parenting, but when he'd tried initiating a game of catch, his son had refused. Without Darcy, Jax remained a no-go with Brody.

When his grandfather came outside, Brody went ballistic with sheer joy. The toddler was glad to see everyone—anyone—but his dad. The optimism Jax had felt only last night faded.

He had a long way to go before he earned Brody's trust. Jax's gaze flitted toward the tree house again. A long way before he regained Darcy's trust, too.

Throughout dinner, his attention wandered. Anna, her husband, Ryan, and their baby daughter had also come for the impromptu cookout. The backyard buzzed with the soft, fluted tones of his mother, sister and Charlie's wife, Evy.

Grandpa Everett had a surprise gift for Brody. His tanned little legs pumping the pedals, Brody rode the new Big Wheel along the brick path. Baby Ruby happily rocked in the baby swing Evy kept for her. Charlie and their dad speculated which pitcher would lead the Nationals to a victorious season.

Jax's thoughts were next door as they'd often been the last summer he lived here. When car lights swept the Parks's driveway, he swallowed against a rush of feeling, refusing to give in to the clamoring of his pulse.

He rested his hands on his stomach, his feet crossed at the ankles, a picture of nonchalance. But he didn't fool his mother. He never had.

Anna's family left soon after. Charlie and his dad went inside to watch the last inning of the game. And Evy begged for the honor of giving Brody a bath before putting him in the Spider-Man pajamas Jax had brought, anticipating a late night out.

No skin off his nose if she wanted to grapple with his son in the bathtub. But Brody would probably be a perfect child for everyone except his father.

Jax started to help his mother clear the table, but she shooed him away. "I got this." Her gaze slid next door. "I'm sure you can think of something to do with yourself for a little while."

It was his mom who'd asked him to go invite the little girl next door to join them for freezer pops that long-ago day. The lime-green had been

Jax's personal favorite, but thereafter, he'd given it up for Darcy.

His mother stacked a few plates. "Probably lots to discuss. Among other things." She gave him a sweet smile. "You two were thick as thieves, especially that last summer."

Jax flushed. His mother had known about that, too? He'd been eager to take on the world. Yet despite his outward bravado, he'd been inwardly conflicted about leaving home. Not unlike most eighteen-year-olds, he supposed.

His mother nudged him. "Back where you began. Best place to start."

Maybe she was right. Maybe if he really hoped to start over, he had to begin where he'd left off. Where everything had unknowingly derailed for him.

Bypassing the abandoned Big Wheel, he stuffed his hands in his pockets as he tromped across the grass. Darcy didn't give herself enough credit. With her get-over-yourself common sense, he'd felt safe confiding his secret fears and aspirations.

He'd told Darcy things he'd never understood about himself until he heard the words coming out of his mouth. She was a good listener, easy to be with and fun.

Still a girl, though, and other than the dude Anna constantly hung out with in those days, his sister's best friend. Anna had eventually found happiness with that dude, Ryan Savage, but only after intense heartache due to the too-young death of her first husband.

Jax wended his way through the stand of crepe myrtles between the driveways. A hint of magnolia perfumed the night air as he stopped at the tree house steps. Widowed like him, Anna had returned home. Unlike him, she'd mourned a truly wonderful marriage.

Guilt struck Jax, shrouding him with the familiar feeling of helpless failure. He stared up into the branches. What he wouldn't give to turn back the clock to the morning he'd reported to basic training. Would his life have been different, if instead of heading out at the crack of dawn, he'd kept his promise? Gone to the tree house? Told Darcy...

He kicked the bottom step, forgetting he wore flip-flops. Pain ricocheted through his big toe.

"Who's there?" Darcy called, her voice sharp.

"Me." Like she'd recognize who "me" was after all these years?

But her head popped over the railing. "What do you want, Jax?"

You...

He sucked in a breath. That couldn't be true. It had been an emotional day, seeing his mom and dad again, after the fiasco with Adrienne's parents. Meeting his little niece, Ruby. Facing the ongoing breach with his son.

"I want..." He cleared his throat. "I want to talk. Can I come up?"

He'd never felt he needed her permission before. Yet now...they weren't the same kids they'd been. He wasn't sure of anything when it came to adult Darcy.

Darcy's lips twisted. "At your own peril, Pruitt." Her head disappeared from view.

A quote they'd borrowed from a movie they'd watched in the days before the cinema on the square closed.

His heart thundering, he took the curving steps two at a time. Stopping at the top, he felt his chest heave. "Hey."

Sunk in a collapsible lawn chair with her bare legs updrawn, Darcy looked at him.

"Y'all have a good outing today?" Sensing that if he waited, he'd never be asked, Jax moved to the empty chair beside her. "I know how you love Mondays."

Abruptly, her feet plunked on the wooden boards. "You wanted to talk, so talk."

Elbows propped on his knees, he knotted his hands. "How 'bout them Nats?"

By the light of the waxing moon, Jax saw her lip curl. He tried again. "About what you said the other day?"

"I say a lot of things, Jax."

"Ain't that the truth," he grunted. "But I'm talking about your assessment of the Pruitt brothers."

"How Charlie is the best looking?" Incredulity

laced her voice. "You came over here to talk to me about that?"

"Among other things." His words were an unconscious echo of his mom's. "For the record, Charlie's Clark Kent good looks are so last century."

"Are they now?" She turned toward the sliver of harbor visible from their perch. "In your humble opinion?"

"In my humble but accurate opinion."

As she stared out over the moon-dappled water, her lips twitched. "What about Ben?"

Jax wrinkled his nose. "Squid Boy?"

"What's not to like about a Navy SEAL?"

He shrugged. "Way overrated."

She swatted at a mosquito. "Unlike Green Berets?"

He grinned.

"There's always Will." She quirked an eyebrow. "What woman doesn't love a firefighter?"

"Helmet Head?" He rolled his eyes. "Who can tell beneath the turnout gear?"

A smile tugged at the corners of her mouth. "You're as impossible as ever, Jax Pruitt. And just as conceited."

"One of the reasons you like me so much."

"You wish." She glared. "What other reasons?"

He settled into the chair with a contented sigh. This was exactly like old times. "For one thing, I make you laugh."

At her very unladylike hoot of derision, his grin slipped.

"I'm not laughing with you, Jaxon. I'm laughing *at* you."

He planted his palms on the armrests of the chair. "Whatever it takes to keep you talking to me, Darce."

She scowled. "Try whatever it takes to keep me from punching you. 'Cause you're overdue, Pruitt."

He offered his cheek. "Go ahead and wallop me one. I deserve it. Get it out of your system."

"Not that you don't deserve it, Jax, but for once let's pretend to be grown-ups."

"I should've written you like I said I would." His voice dropped.

Except for the thrumming of the cicadas, silence stretched between them. His palms began to sweat.

Finally, "Why didn't you write, Jax?"

The easier of his promises to explain. Both of them were desperately dancing around his other broken promise to her on that long-ago morning.

He wiped his hands on his shorts. "It wasn't like the war stories Grandpa told about his army career."

Stories Jax realized now had been highly redacted versions of what his grandfather must've experienced at D-day and on the Korean Peninsula.

He took a deep breath. "Boot camp took everything I had to remain focused. The sergeant did his best to break us."

She studied his face. "And you, being Jax, were determined not to be broken."

But like the rest, he'd broken eventually. So Uncle Sam could rebuild them into soldiers who could survive what lay ahead.

"And then I deployed."

"But still you never wrote." Her voice grew pensive. "Do you know I've spent fourteen years not watching the evening news, Jax?"

How could he make sense of this for her? How could he make sense of this for himself? "You didn't belong to that world, Darce."

A world as far removed from the peaceful oasis of Kiptohanock as the earth from the stars overhead. The world that ultimately took Adrienne's life. A world that needed to remain separate from the one that mattered to him. The real him.

When Darcy touched his arm, he jumped.

"Jax?"

And like that, she recalled him from the edge of the emptiness he'd felt since losing his wife.

"If you ever want to tell someone, I'll listen."

"If I could ever tell anyone…" His voice wobbled. "I'd tell you."

For the space of a heartbeat, he feared she'd insist he come clean, but instead she threw him a lifeline. "What else did you want to discuss, Jax?"

On stable footing once more, he outlined his

idea to reach out to disabled veterans with a kayaking program designed to overcome their disabilities.

"Not a bad idea, Jaxon Pruitt. It has real possibilities."

"I knew a guy once..." He blew out a breath.

Somehow, they'd ventured onto dangerous terrain again.

"Is he okay?"

Jax shifted. "After his injury, he lost the will to live. He didn't make it."

"I'm sorry, Jax." She didn't press him for details.

"A day out on the water once in a while might've given him the courage to live another day."

She squeezed his hand. "With the VA hospital across the bay, I think your program stands a good chance of succeeding."

He held on to her hand.

Frowning, she pulled away. "Glad we could come to a meeting of the minds."

Whereas he would like to come to a meeting of so much more. Namely, her lips.

He nearly gasped out loud. Where had that come from? This was Darcy. As if he needed reminding. Which, judging from his pounding heart, he did.

Something in his expression must've changed because her eyes widened. He took a moment to drown in the blue-green of her gaze. And without intending to, he leaned closer. Her lips parted.

Jax reached to cup her face and…he dropped his hand. What was he doing? Confusion written across her features, she sat back.

His Adam's apple bobbed. "Sorry. I didn't mean to do that."

"Flirting is just so instinctual to you, isn't it?" Her nostrils flared. "Kind of like breathing to the rest of us."

But far better he tick her off than the alternative. Therein lay only ruin for both of them. "Don't take it personally. I've sworn off women."

She actually snorted.

"I'm serious, Darcy. I'm no good at love."

"You plan to remain single for the rest of your life? You?" She smirked. "Jaxon Delano Pruitt?"

He jutted his jaw. "Yes. I do."

She flung out her hand. "Fish gotta swim. Birds gotta fly, Jax."

He shook his head. "I plan to devote myself to being Brody's father."

"At the risk of sounding like my mother, do finding love and raising a child have to be mutually exclusive?"

"Considering what happened with Adrienne—" He clamped his jaw tight. "It's better for everyone if I stick to my plan."

"As usual, you're full of plans, aren't you?" She

pursed her lips. "And I'll believe it when I see it. You are the biggest flirt I've ever met."

"Maybe just with you."

She came out of her chair, fists balled. "Just with me?" Her eyes flashed. "Because I'm safe? Because I'm so out of the realm of real possibility?"

"I didn't mean…" Rising, he crossed his arms. "Why is every conversation with you full of land mines?"

"Which only proves Labor Day can't come soon enough for me, Jax Pruitt."

"Right back at you, sister."

She vibrated. "I'm not your sister."

He lifted his chin. "I've always been well aware of that fact."

Darcy charged toward the steps, then whirled and came back again. "Here's something else for you to ponder, Pruitt. We're stuck working with each other for the next few months. But don't, I repeat, don't—" her finger jabbed into his chest, punctuating her words "—mess with me."

"*I* can do peaceful coexistence. Can you, Darce?"

"Me? You are so…" She stomped down the stairs, muttering vastly uncomplimentary things about his personhood.

He raked his hand over his face. Coexistence maybe. Peaceful, though, wasn't a word he'd use to describe him and Darcy.

Another more dangerous word leaped to mind. Which he immediately rejected. A place he couldn't afford to go. Not after his track record with Adrienne. Not when it came to Darcy.

Chapter Five

Tuesday morning, Darcy didn't feel up to dealing with more mixed signals from Jax. So she texted him that she'd meet him late afternoon for the sunset paddle. Leaving him in the capable hands of the hometown college kids she'd already hired as the first week of the summer season kicked off.

He didn't reply. She knew that because she kept her cell turned on. In case Savannah or Ozzie or Chas needed her. Right... She'd just keep telling herself that.

With her dad putting together next Sunday's sermon in the study—doing the usual floor pacing—and her mom headed to a guild meeting at the church, Darcy found herself at loose ends. She disliked having free time on her hands. But with Jax Pruitt's return, more than her schedule had gone out the window.

Thoughts of what almost happened last night

clattered around inside her head. She should be ecstatic nothing had happened. Should be… Right?

With her untapped energy near flash point, she decided to power wash the driveway. She'd reached the three-quarter mark when a blue RAV4 pulled in next door. Darcy turned off the machine, her ears ringing from the deafening noise.

Anna hopped out. "How do you like my new wheels?" she shouted.

Darcy laid down the hose. "I thought you might choose red this time." Anna's favorite color.

The blue color was the only similarity the RAV4 shared with the vintage VW Beetle Anna had driven since high school. But the Bug had met a watery demise on Christmas Eve.

Darcy's bare feet squelched across the wet pavement as she walked to the Pruitt side. "Is the world's most fabulous baby inside this new ride of yours?"

Anna laughed, tucking her long, straight brown hair behind her ear. "We've been shopping in Onancock."

Darcy wiped her hands on the backside of her shorts and poked her head through the open passenger door. "Hey, Ruby Dooby. Y'all here to see Grandma Gail?"

Recognizing her voice, the dark-haired baby with her late father's Latino coloring smiled so widely her dark eyes went into crescent moons. Thrilling her honorary Aunt Darcy.

"Actually…" Anna flipped her hair over her shoulder "…we're here to see you. Unless you'd rather we come back after you're finished power washing."

"Please stay. I'd love an excuse to quit."

Ruby's little arms reached for her, but Darcy hesitated. "Maybe you should get her out, Anna. I'm soaking wet. I don't want to get her dirty."

"It's you she wants to see, Darcy."

Ruby strained forward as far as the straps allowed.

"Okay, you've been warned." But secretly pleased, Darcy made short work of the buckles and picked her up.

Cupping her hand on top of Ruby's head as she backed out of the vehicle, Darcy closed her eyes for a second. Savoring the feel of the child in her arms. Inhaling the clean scent of her baby shampoo.

Darcy felt her heart speed up, recalling the endearing sweetness of Jax's son, Brody. For despite what she'd said to her mother, if Darcy's situation had been different, she would've so wanted a child of her own. Jax's child?

She gritted her teeth. If there was one thing she'd learned from her father's melancholy, it was that there was no point wishing for what you couldn't have. And she stuffed that idle musing into the dark recesses of never-gonna-happen.

Ruby in her arms, she headed to the broad-planked porch of the parsonage. She and Anna sank into the pair of rocking chairs flanking a pot of hot-pink dahlias.

Her feet planted flat on the weathered boards and Ruby on her lap, she set the rocker in motion. "I cannot believe this little girl is almost six months old."

Anna's brown eyes—uncomfortably like her brother Jax's—lit up. "A lot of water under that proverbial bridge, right?"

Darcy laughed.

They could laugh now, but only because of the subsequent happy ending. Anna's car had slid off one of the many bridges spanning the tidal estuaries during an ice storm. Stranding widowed Anna—heavily in labor—until she was rescued by her former high school sweetheart, Ryan Savage. In February, Darcy and Evy had served as bridesmaids when Anna and Ryan finally tied the knot.

"Is Ryan at the district office today?"

Ruby reached for the gold hoop dangling from Darcy's ear. Wincing, Darcy removed her carring from the baby's surprisingly tenacious grip.

Anna handed her jingling car keys to her long-awaited, much-loved daughter. "His new job as the coordinator for at-risk students finally enabled us to buy a new vehicle."

"Will you teach at the elementary school next fall?"

"Ryan wants me to be a stay-at-home mother to Ruby. At least until she starts kindergarten."

"Oh, Anna…" Darcy bounced Ruby on her lap, earning a baby giggle. "I know how much this means to you."

"And who knows?" Anna sat forward, her hands laced together on her knees. "Ruby might find herself with a sibling or two in the meantime."

"That would be wonderful."

Anna's brown eyes pooled. "You of all people understand what a long road it was for Ryan and me."

Darcy's eyes misted, too. "I'm so, so happy for you, dear friend."

And she was. Anna and Ryan's happily-ever-after had been wrought only after a great deal of pain.

"But—" Anna rapped her palms of the armrests of the rocker "—I came over here to talk about you."

Darcy looked up from razzing Ruby's neck with her lips. "Me?"

"You and my brother."

"I guess you heard about his buyout of the business." Darcy stilled at a sudden unwelcome thought. "You probably knew about it before I did."

Anna leaned across the dahlias to touch Darcy's arm. "I only knew he was coming home."

Some of the betrayal Darcy had felt since Saturday seeped away. It had hurt thinking everyone was in on this except for her.

"I know how much you wanted the Kiptohanock shop, Darcy. I understand how strange it must be with Jax coming home."

Darcy shook her head. "I'll manage."

Sixteen-year-old Anna had proved herself a true friend when Jax left for Basic. Loyalty counted for a lot in Darcy's experience.

Anna blew out a breath. "Jax says Brody has formed quite a connection with you."

Darcy really, really didn't want to spend a perfectly fine Tuesday morning talking about Anna's brother. Not when she was doing her best not to see him—much less think about him.

"I guess you also heard I'm leaving come Labor Day." She gave Anna a brittle smile. "Exiled. Banished."

"Although I realize everything seems wrong to you..." Anna covered Darcy's hand with hers. "Despite evidence to the contrary, I have faith it will all turn out right in the end."

Darcy's eyes stung. "Will it?" Jax had said almost the exact same words Saturday night.

"For you. For Jax. And for Brody, too." Anna's voice hitched. "Somehow. Some way. Remember what your dad says."

Darcy grimaced. "You mean, if it's not right, then it's not the end?"

Anna squeezed her hand. "Hang in there, sweet

sister of my heart. I truly believe God has beautiful plans for your life."

Plans? Anna sounded like her brother. And Darcy would like to tell Jax Pruitt once and for all what he could do with his so-called plans...

A suspicious, warm moisture dampened Darcy's thighs. "Uh, Anna..." She extended Ruby toward her mother. "I think we may have a situation."

"That'll teach me to buy the cheapest diapers in the store." Anna rose. "Sorry about that."

Darcy followed her off the porch. "No problem. By the time I finish the driveway, I'll be good as new."

"Be that as it may..."

They stepped between the fuchsia-flamed crepe myrtles.

"Be that as it may what?"

After opening the hatch, Anna laid her daughter on the carpeted mat. "Would you get the diaper bag out of the backseat for me?"

Darcy moved around to the passenger side.

Anna untaped the diaper on her wiggly infant. "Believe me when I tell you how much my parents and I appreciate the sacrifices you're making for Brody and Jax."

Silent, Darcy passed the diaper bag over the headrest.

Anna made short work of changing the diaper. "Jax feels bad about the position he's put you in unintentionally."

In view of what almost happened last night, Darcy decided not to share her thoughts on Jax's supposed intentionality. But her expression must've given her away.

"No, I mean it, Darcy. He's always had a special feeling for you."

Darcy squared her shoulders. "Seriously?"

Anna encircled Ruby's small, waving feet with one hand. "I am serious. Jax likes tough, strong women like you." She pressed Ruby's heels against her lips.

Darcy's mouth twisted. "I'm nothing like his totally gorgeous, kick-butt soldier wife, Adrienne."

"True."

Darcy rocked back.

"But I mean that in the best possible sense." Anna met her gaze head-on. "Adrienne and Jax weren't happy, Darcy."

That was a news flash. And something inside Darcy ached at the thought of Jax unhappy.

She lifted her chin. "Jax claims he's sworn off women."

"Like that's going to happen," sniffed his sister.

She exchanged smirks with Anna. "That's what I said."

Lifting Ruby, Anna settled the child in her arms. "So there's no good reason not to see what God intends for the both of you this summer."

"You sound like my mother."

"Who is a very wise woman," Anna reminded her, before placing Ruby in her car seat and driving away.

But later that afternoon by the time she arrived at the shop, Darcy had managed to come up with a dozen reasons why working with Jaxon Pruitt was a mistake. Out back, she found him running through warm-up exercises with the honeymooning couple.

In waterproof Chaco sandals, Jax placed his hands against the dock pylon. Extending one long leg behind him, he demonstrated how to stretch the hamstring muscle. And during the torso rotation, his T-shirt clung to his tight abs. Her cheeks flamed when he caught her staring.

Jax helped the bride into a tandem sea kayak. On the water in her hot pink Squamish kayak, Darcy went through the last paddle instructions with the honeymooners, while Jax eased into the lime-green NDK Explorer he'd chosen, based on fit and maneuverability.

With the kayaks gathered in a semicircle, she dipped her paddle into the murky water and led the way, single file. Jax would bring up the rear. Hugging the shoreline, Darcy kept their caravan of kayaks clear of marina traffic. Navigating the half-moon harbor could be tricky. She always breathed a sigh of relief upon rounding the point. The channel widened as they paddled the inter-coastal waterway. Every now and again she paused, paddle resting across her lap, and drew their attention to various sights. A derelict oyster shucking facility, long past its heyday. The ruins of a village on a distant barrier island.

"A town out here?" The bride's eyes grew large. "Talk about isolated."

Darcy relayed a few stories she'd learned from her father about what life had been like for the families who'd fished the sea in a bygone era.

The groom, a Navy corpsman stationed in Norfolk, shook his head. "Why was the village abandoned?"

Jax answered before Darcy could. "The Chesapeake hurricane of 1933 forced the locals off the islands and onto the peninsula."

The bride shivered. "Does anyone still live there?"

Jax leaned forward in his kayak. "Most of the barrier islands are owned by conservation organizations now."

Pointing out a snowy egret rising from the cattails, Darcy picked up her paddle again. The route narrowed as she headed through the salt marsh into a winding creek, a constricting tunnel of green cordgrass, like a maze with its hairpin twists and turns. She hung back to make sure the honeymooners negotiated one of the sharp curves.

"We'll take a break soon," she said encouragingly. "It's not far."

Her arms went into the rhythmic push-pull, right-left rotation. Nearing the exposed portion of sand, she leaped out of the kayak into the water. Pulling her boat onto the muddy embankment, she turned to assist the honeymooners. But having beached his kayak, Jax dragged the tandem craft ashore and held it steady as the bride extricated herself.

The young woman plodded through the calf-high water. "That was fun."

Darcy smiled. "Looks like y'all were getting the hang of it."

"We passed the test." Joining his wife on the beach, the groom planted a kiss on her lips. "Probably should've taken the kayak trip before we tied the knot."

Darcy helped Jax stow the paddles out of reach of the incoming tide. "What test?"

"The canoe test." The corpsman grinned. "Or in this case, the kayak test. I've always heard the best future indicator of a relationship is a canoe trip."

Darcy planted her hands on her hips. "How do you mean?"

The bride smiled. "It reveals how a couple will handle challenges."

Jax tilted his head. "Like working in tandem to navigate strong currents or unexpected hazards."

The groom placed his arm around his wife's slim waist. "How they resolve power struggles, too."

Darcy shot Jax a look. "The old 'I'll steer, you paddle' routine?"

His lips quirked. "Long as one of them doesn't jump out of the canoe and throw a paddle at the other."

The bride chuckled. "And not get sucked into the blame game."

Jax sobered. "The biggest thing might be the ability to just stay in the canoe. To not get out and quit."

Was he speaking from bitter personal experience?

Darcy couldn't bear the look on his face. "Maybe we should start promoting problem-solving excursions to engaged couples."

"Happily-ever-after paddling." The bride laughed. "I love it."

Jax's eyebrow cocked. "A test of mutual trust, eh, Darce?"

She didn't answer, instead taking the faint trail to the other side of the dune. She waded into the Atlantic, the ocean water cold against her ankles. The honeymooners followed.

For their inspection, Jax held up the hermit crab he'd plucked from a tidal pool. At his smile, Darcy felt her stomach tighten in a familiar way, but the crab withdrew into its shell. Like her with Jax?

The couple strolled along the seashore, beachcombing. To her delight, the bride found a nearly intact conch shell, half buried in the sand. Jax pointed out oyster half shells and mussels that had washed ashore.

How would she and Jax fare in the same kayak? Could they work together? Was it time to stop fighting the current?

Standing next to Jax, she watched the glowing sun sink lower in the sky. Farther down the beach, the honeymooners nestled in each other's arms. With a sudden burst of orange and gold, the sun disappeared behind the western horizon.

Jax snatched up a shell and hurled it into the foaming waves. "Mom's worried about Brody. She says he needs to learn how to swim."

"Don't you think he ought to?" Darcy's toes sank deep into the sand as she resisted the pull of the tide. Not unlike how she felt when Jax looked at her. "Brody lives on a peninsula surrounded on three sides by water. And there's the tidal creek in your backyard."

"I agree, but he doesn't trust me." Jax stared out over the choppy water toward the deepening hues of lavender and indigo in the sky. "He wouldn't let me teach him. He's still only two. Maybe next summer."

"Let me teach him." Where had that come from?

Jax's brow furrowed. "I couldn't ask you to do that for me."

"You're not asking. I'm offering."

So much for her planned avoidance of all things

Jaxon Pruitt. But when had her path with Jax ever been easy or straightforward?

"Midafternoons the shop is pretty quiet. Tell your mom to bring him by tomorrow."

His eyes darted as if he was searching for an excuse to refuse.

She jutted her jaw. "I lifeguarded at the Y, Jax. I'm certified in baby aquatics. Brody's safe with me."

"It's not that, Darce. It's just..."

She angled her head. "Of course, I'd need you to help me with his lessons."

His eyes became hooded. "You think this might bring Brody and me closer?"

Yeah, that. She nodded at the reminder. This summer was about Jax and Brody finding their way to each other.

This was *not* about her and Jax. Merely the sort of thing people did for one another in Kiptohanock. Neighbor helping neighbor. Although technically, they no longer lived next door to each other.

But her dad would be proud of her for helping Brody. Right up a PK's alley. Her mom would be jubilant for Darcy to spend more time with father and son. Especially elated about the Jax part.

Jax scrutinized her. "If you're sure."

"I'm sure. Hopefully, Brody will be interested."

"A chance to spend more time with his beloved

Dawcy?" Jax's mouth twitched. "Who could turn down an offer like that?"

She didn't bother to point out history had already proved him a liar on that score. "You should round up the newlyweds. We'd better head back while we still have light." She trudged over the dune and took a deep, fortifying breath.

Because in reality, she wasn't sure of anything. Never had been when it came to Jax Pruitt. More likely than not, she'd find herself in over her head. And everybody knew what happened to people in over their heads.

Eventually, they drowned.

Chapter Six

The next week flew by as Jax did a crash course in learning the business. He worked overtime to keep up with Darcy, physically and mentally. But despite her best efforts, the breach remained between him and Brody.

Jax hadn't failed to note, though, how she went out of her way to avoid him during work hours. Which rankled, despite the fact it'd been him who pushed her away that night in the tree house.

Each afternoon, his mother dropped Brody off at the shop. And Darcy made it her business to initiate his son into the joys of a life lived on the water. Splashing, playing, having fun. But no worries.

From the start, Brody proved himself a fish, jumping without hesitation into her outstretched arms. Immediately sticking his whole head into the water. Darcy grabbed Brody up, but not before nearly giving both her and Jax a coronary.

Sitting on the dock keeping his distance, Jax felt his chest swell with pride as he watched his son's little legs scissor kick, slicing through the water. As for Darcy?

Feet dangling over the water, Jax decided annoying was preferable to indifference. "He's a natural, like his father," he called. Just to get a rise out of her.

"If anything, he's a SEAL in the making." Her mouth quirked. "Like his uncle Ben."

Standing in the waist-deep water, she kept a firm arm around Brody's midsection, keeping him afloat as he blew bubbles. "Come on in with us, Jax."

"Ben can get his own son." Jax slipped off the dock, flinching as the water hit his bare skin.

She laughed. "If Ben ever comes home, Shore girls might just take you up on that offer."

Easing toward them, Jax stopped in his tracks mid-motion. "Including you?"

An unwelcome notion—Darcy with any of his brothers. She'd spent her childhood playing with Anna and Jax and... Ben.

The Kiptohanock Four, Dad called them. Surely Jax hadn't been out of the loop that long? Surely his mom would've clued him in?

Going deeper, he moved toward Darcy, the water sluicing around him. Darcy and Ben? Nah... Unlikely in the extreme. Though opposites did attract. Him and Adrienne, case in point.

And look where that had landed them both. His feet sank into the sandy bottom. Miserable.

Sunlight glinted off the red tints in Darcy's hair. The red she didn't like to acknowledge. She'd never be interested in serious Ben. Would she? Jax figured her type to be someone more fun-loving. Like him. He gulped.

He started forward again, but she halted him with her hand. "Stay there. I want to try something with Brody." She bent over his son, murmuring instructions as Brody dog-paddled.

Jax had always sort of considered her his exclusive territory. Which was crazy. But watching her with his son, he felt something in his chest tighten.

He didn't own her. She didn't belong to him. She never had. But to the best of his knowledge, she wasn't in a relationship. How could she be, considering the hours she worked at the shop?

"That's right, Brody," Darcy encouraged as she put his son through the paces. She sputtered when Brody's scooped palm accidentally splashed her in the face.

Swiping her hand over her eyes, she laughed. Dewy drops of water spiked her lashes. And Jax's insides went cattywampus.

Was there someone she waited for? Was Ben the reason she'd never married? Why hadn't some Shore guy snapped her up already? Darcy Parks, honest to a fault, was a treasure. And the idea of

Darcy with Ben—or anyone else on the planet—
didn't set well with Jax.

He cleared his throat. "You looking forward to
Ben's return, Darcy?"

A wave lapped over her shoulders, and she did
a little hop to keep her footing. "It'd be good to
see Ben, but I'll probably be in the Keys."

He glared. Like he needed another reminder
of her impending departure at summer's end. All
week she'd gotten calls about apartment rentals
from Aunt Shirley. Fast becoming his not-favor-
ite aunt. And a dude from a trekking company in
Alabama had phoned three times.

"This kid is all you, Jax." She sucked in a breath
as she almost lost her grip on Dolphin Boy. "But
a little fear is a good thing."

"Go big or go home, Darce." Like he was one
to talk.

"Hold on there, Brody." She scooped his son
into her arms, resting his swimsuit-clad bottom
against her hip. "I want you to swim to Daddy."

Brody's brows puckered. "No."

Jax bit his lip.

"Please, Brody," she cajoled, as the water
dripped off his son's bare torso. "Let's show
Daddy how much you've learned."

But Brody stiffened, his arms in a stranglehold
around her neck.

Jax's heart sank. "It's okay, Darce."

She ran her hand over Brody's hair, plastered to his head. "I'll be right here the whole time." She kissed his forehead. "There's nothing to be scared of."

Brody shook his head violently. Wrapping his legs around Darcy, he clung to her like a limpet on a stone.

Jax wanted to weep. "He's not scared, Darcy. He just doesn't trust me. I—I don't want to force him." His voice broke. "You can't make somebody love you."

Something fierce shone in Darcy's eyes. For a second, he thought... But she dropped her gaze and whispered in Brody's ear.

Brody lifted his head, scowling at his father. But whatever she'd said to him, he slowly unpeeled himself from her, first his legs, then his arms. He eased into the water, Darcy holding him underneath his armpits.

"Stay there, Jax. Brody's going to swim to you."

"Darcy, he doesn't have—"

"He's going to do it." Her gaze locked on to his. "Trust me."

Jax opened his arms, baring his chest. "If there's anyone in the whole world I trust, Darcy, it's you."

Her smile lit places in his heart he'd believed long dead.

"It's go time, Brode." She leaned over his son,

holding him against the lapping current. "One, two, three…"

Brody took off like one of the NASA rockets at Wallops Island.

Darcy bobbed in the water, clapping. "Go, Brody, go."

Jax held his breath, willing his son to come to him. "I'll catch you, Brody." He extended his hands. "I've got you."

Within a few strokes, Brody was there, and Jax swept him into his arms. "You did it, Brody. You did it, son."

Jax hugged him to his chest, water streaming off the both of them. How good it felt to hold his child close. At least for this one moment.

"Yay for Brody!" Darcy fist-pumped the air.

Grinning, Brody lifted his own skinny arm. "Yay me."

Jax bounced him in the water. "Yay you."

Brody wriggled, trying to get free. "Me do again."

"Farther this time, Brode?" At his vigorous nod, Darcy moved back another yard.

When Jax carefully released him, Brody took off toward her.

"Thank you, Darcy." Over the splashing, Jax's eyes locked on to hers. "I think maybe he's beginning to trust me a little."

Catching Brody in her arms, she whirled. His

little legs flew out behind him, skimming the surface of the water.

"Whee!" His son squirmed. "Do again. Swim, Dawcy."

"Jax, go back a ways." She motioned and set Brody down.

His boy took off at once, and the joy in Jax's heart couldn't be measured. It filled him, spilling out of him. Back and forth Brody swam, Jax and Darcy wearing out long before his energetic son.

Eventually, Darcy called it quits. With Brody on her hip, she trudged toward the beach, Jax following. On solid ground, she placed Brody on his feet. He tore off toward the supply shed, where he pulled out his favorite toddler-size orange PFD.

"What did you say to him, Darce? What made him agree to swim to me?"

Keeping her eye on Brody threading his arms through the life jacket, she smiled. "I told him if he swam to you, I'd teach him how to do a wet exit."

"Darcy! He's a two-year-old."

Her shoulders shook. "I know. But he's seen us teaching paddle school, and he thinks it would be fun to get dunked under the water. What we have here is a burgeoning daredevil."

Jax raked his hand over his head.

"Now you know how your mom felt. Fear is so not a factor for your little guy, Jaxon Pruitt." She patted his biceps. "I wouldn't let him watch extreme sports on television anytime soon."

She headed up the incline toward Brody, who was doing his best to lug a child-size kayak to the water. "And over the next few years, if I were you, Jax," she called over her shoulder, "I'd be sure and keep my insurance up-to-date."

One benefit of afternoon swim lessons was that by suppertime, Brody was worn-out. Out like a light by eight o'clock without protest. Both good and bad, from Jax's perspective.

Good that he had some time to himself. Bad in that it gave him more time to think, and more time alone. Though being alone, and savaged by guilt, was exactly what Jax deserved.

And then there was the continuing battle to keep Darcy out of his mind. Like how the sun kissed the freckles on her nose when they were in the marsh. The strength of her arms paddling across the tidal creeks. Or her kindness in trying to restore his son to him.

She was pretty wonderful. He lived to make her laugh. To see her eyes light up. To catch her gazing at him. To simply, under any circumstances, spend time with her.

Foolish, futile thoughts going round and round in his head. Toward a destination he couldn't sanction. Not considering how he'd failed the only other woman in his life.

So one night, after Brody had been put to bed, it was with some relief he opened the door to his brother Charlie. Jax was glad for the distraction and the company. As the oldest, already soldiering in global hot spots, he'd missed his youngest brother's growing-up years.

But the tallest, burliest of his siblings had done well for himself. A distinguished deputy sheriff, he'd reopened their renovated childhood home to Pruitt family members for however long they wanted or needed to stay. Including their happily retired, world traveler parents.

"You've been sent by Mom to check on me, haven't you?"

Charlie lolled against the door frame. "She's worried about her firstborn."

Jax stepped aside to let him through. "I'm doing okay."

Charlie sidled into the kitchen. "Are you?"

He yanked open the refrigerator. "I can offer you sweet tea, water or…sweet tea."

Charlie propped his elbows on the counter. "I got all the sweet tea I need at home, bro." He gave Jax that Cheshire cat smile of his.

Jax rolled his eyes. "Water it is then." He pulled out a bottle. "You married up, my friend."

"Yeah." Charlie smirked, taking the bottle. "I did."

Jax grabbed a water bottle for himself. "How's that book club thing working out for you, Charles? Whatcha reading now?" He chortled. *"Gone with the Wind?"*

Charlie unscrewed the cap. "Like you'd know *Gone with the Wind* from a comic book." He threw back his head and took a swig. Coming up for air, he wiped his hand across his mouth. "But for your information, book club doesn't meet during the summer."

Jax opened the French doors to the deck. "All kidding aside, I'm happy for you, Charlie. You're a lucky man."

His brother sank into one of the deck chairs. "Not lucky, blessed."

Jax sat down, glancing over the railing toward the gurgling creek. From somewhere, the scent of gardenias wafted. The two of them remained silent for a few moments, enjoying the dark summer evening.

Until Charlie worked up the nerve to say what he'd come to say. "You've been happier this summer than I've seen you in a long time, Jax."

Because of Darcy. Jax took another sip of water. But he couldn't say that to his brother. "How 'bout those Nats?"

Not easily distracted, Charlie could be like a terrier with a bone. "Adrienne's been dead almost two years, Jax."

Jax set the water bottle on the small table between them. "I'm not having this conversation with you." He'd spent most of the last two years trying *not* to think about Adrienne.

Charlie ran his finger around the lip of his own plastic bottle. "When then? And with whom?"

Jax knotted his hands in his lap. "So the family elected you, huh?"

Charlie sighed. "Her dying wasn't your fault, bro."

Jax clenched his jaw. "I know that."

His brother's eyes locked on to his. "Do you?"

"What happened before she died *was* my fault." Jax balled his fist. "And every day I see what the loss of her has done to Brody."

Charlie leaned forward. "The guilt is eating you alive. And you're stuck on punishing yourself. Not allowing yourself a chance for happiness."

"Happiness?" Jax's mouth twisted. "Not part of my plan. I've got a new business to operate and a son to raise. Brody needs me."

Charlie rested his elbows on his knees. "What Brody needs is a mom. And you're too busy guilt-tripping yourself to see who is right under your nose."

Jax gaped at him. "What're you talking about?"

"I'm talking about Darcy. You spend a lot of time with a woman you claim not to care about."

Jax stiffened. "I do care about Darcy. She's a friend."

Charlie snorted. "Tell me another one, bro."

"We work together." Jax dropped his gaze. "Anything good happening between my son and me is her doing. And without her help in the business, I'd already be in over my head."

Charlie laid his palms on the wooden armrests. "She's more to you than you'll admit. Don't deny it, Jax."

Jax's shoulders slumped. "Even if she was, how could I bring another woman into our lives when I failed Brody's mother so miserably?"

There was the crux of it. He'd made mistakes, but the biggest mistake had been trusting Adrienne. She'd taken his heart and crushed it.

"Adrienne did a number on your head, Jax," his brother whispered in the darkness. "I get why you'd be scared."

Jax straightened. "Don't blame Adrienne. I was as much to blame for what happened as she was." He gritted his teeth. "And I'm *not* scared."

Charlie blew out a breath. "Somehow you've got to forgive yourself and let go of what happened."

Jax scrubbed a hand over his face. "I don't deserve forgiveness, Charlie."

"None of us do, Jax, but God forgives us anyway. And He has a way of working everything out to our good if we allow Him to." Charlie's voice softened. "Evy and I are a prime example of that. I hate to see you lose the best thing, besides Brody, that has ever happened to you."

Jax tilted his head. "What're you talking about?"

"I'm talking about Darcy, bro."

Hopeless futility rose in his throat. "There is no

me and Darcy. There can't ever be. Even if I..." He swallowed. "Darcy barely tolerates me. She doesn't think of me that way."

Emptiness consumed him, as he thought of what he could never have—a life full of love. Not just with any woman, but with the only one he'd ever imagined trusting with his heart, his life and his son—Darcy.

"I wouldn't be too sure, Jax."

He grunted. "She likes me so much she can't wait to move away."

"Did you ever think maybe Darcy's running as scared as you?" Charlie frowned. "Dude, don't let that girl paddle out of your life for Florida. You've got to do something to convince her to stay."

Jax's gut churned. "Fact is, Charlie, if I really care about Darcy, I'll let her—encourage her to— get as far away from me as she can, for her own sake. I'm not marriage material. I'll only hurt her. She deserves better than me."

An incontrovertible truth.

"I think you're off base about Darcy."

"Let it go, Charles," he growled.

"Okay then, let's talk about you." Charlie reached for his water bottle again. "Haven't seen you in church yet."

Jax fidgeted. He'd been meaning to take Brody, but like navigating the turbulent waters of his marriage to Adrienne, it had been easier not to make unnecessary waves when it came to his relationship or lack of relationship with God. "Don't you need to get home to Evy, Charlie?"

No surprise, Charlie stuck to his guns. "Have you tried praying about the guilt? About Darcy?"

Jax stiffened. "No."

"Then what have you got to lose? And how much more could you gain?" Charlie pushed to his feet. "If nothing else, peace."

Peace instead of cold numbness? Wisdom instead of confusion? Was Charlie right?

Jax raked his fingers through his hair. "I'll think about what you said."

"We love you and Brody, Jax." Undemonstrative like all the Pruitts, nevertheless Charlie hugged him, startling Jax. As did his next words. "I suspect Darcy might love you, too."

Jax's heart thudded. That wasn't true. It wasn't.

Charlie moved down the steps. "But don't forget God loves you and Brody more than we ever could."

Jax escorted him around the corner of the house as Charlie headed for his truck, then lifted his hand as his brother drove away.

Was Charlie right? Maybe it was time to stop relying on his own limited strength and reach out to the One whose strength was limitless.

As for Darcy? No matter the yearnings of his stubborn heart, Jax needed to steer clear of any emotional entanglements. Truth was, his heart couldn't take another loss.

Chapter Seven

The next morning, with Brody's hand clasped in his, Jaxon hesitated at the church steps. He craned his neck, gazing up at the white steeple piercing the azure sky. It had been a long time since he'd darkened a church doorway. Adrienne had preferred to spend their few Sundays together leisurely.

Brow puckered, Brody's head swiveled from the harbor to the kayak shop down the block, then past the gazebo on the village green to the church. "What this pwace?"

"This is church, Brody."

Brody's eyebrows scrunched. "What's chuwch?"

Jax winced. "Church. Chuh-rrr-ch."

Brody scowled and pressed his lips together.

Jax let the *r*'s go for now. "Church is one of the places we find God." He squeezed his eyes shut momentarily. "Where we find love. And where love finds us."

Was he talking to Brody or himself?

"I know God." Brody nodded. "Gwandma 'sp-wain to me."

Jax's mom. Thank God for his parents. They'd stood in the gap for him. As Brody's father, he should've been there for his son and hadn't.

After Charlie left last night, Jax had spent a long night thinking. He needed something and someone far more powerful than his own puny efforts to make a new life for his son. To forge a lasting bond with Brody.

Brody tugged him up the steps and inside. Jax paused on the threshold, giving his eyes time to adjust. And to settle his nerves.

This prodigal had been a long time coming home. In more ways than one. He'd done so many things wrong. As a husband and as a father. Was it too late? Too late for Brody and him?

With all his heart, he hoped not. But coming to church had to be the first step in their new start. The first step in the long journey back to his Heavenly Father.

"Jaxon!" Arms outstretched, Reverend Harold Parks hurried down the main aisle of the sanctuary.

He found himself engulfed in the sixtysome-thing pastor's embrace. When Darcy's dad pulled back, Jax spotted tears in his sea-green eyes. Eyes that forcibly reminded him of Darcy.

"Good to see you here today, son." The reverend clapped his shoulder. "So good." Harold Parks bent to Brody's height. "And who's this good-looking young man with you?"

Smiling, Agnes Parks bustled forward. "Isn't he the spitting image of a certain Jaxon Pruitt at that age, Harold?"

Out of breath, Darcy clambered into the foyer. "Sorry I'm late, Dad." Her features altered. "Oh, I didn't expect to see you..."

Jax couldn't tell if seeing them made her happy or sad. Crouching to Brody's height, she gave him a big hug. Okay, clearly pleased to see his son. Jax, not so much.

Brody hung on to her like she was his last, great hope.

Jax understood the appeal. Her cheeks flushed, she looked pretty cute in a white cotton skirt and pink flip-flops. He'd liked to believe the sparkle in her eyes was because of him, but he knew better.

She flicked Brody a quick smile. No smile for him. "Did you come with Grandma Gail to church, Brody?"

It galled Jax that she assumed he needed his mother's help. True, until today. "No, he came— we came alone. Mom and Dad will be here later."

Thrusting her tongue in her cheek, a tiny smile hovered on her lips. And he realized he wasn't the only one who could push buttons.

Jax did a quick scan of the rapidly filling sanctuary. Life in the beach community was casual—

no ties or suits here. Even the reverend wore a golf shirt and slacks.

He liked Darcy's attire, not that he'd ever have the nerve to tell her so. The very feminine, rose-pink, billowy blouse brought out the red in her strawberry blonde hair.

An observation she wouldn't appreciate. A button he decided not to push, since it was Sunday. Not with her playing the proper PK and all.

She took his son's hand. "This is my dad, Brody. You've met my mom already."

Jax nodded. "Miss Agnes made the yummy lasagna."

When Brody smiled, Jax's heart almost split in two. Despite how much Brody resembled him, bittersweet traces of Adrienne lingered in his son's lopsided grin.

Agnes touched Brody's hair. "I learned a long time ago the way to a boy's heart."

"Me hungwy."

Jax frowned. "We just ate breakfast." Brody would have the Parks family believing his father never fed him.

Agnes's lips twitched. "He's a growing boy, Jaxon."

The reverend winked at Brody. "I promise to make the service as short as the Lord allows, young Pruitt."

Jax stepped out of the doorway as the Duers entered the sanctuary. Bristly mustached waterman Seth Duer patted Jax's arm. "Good to have you home, Jaxon."

He moved Brody aside as a trickle of Seth Duer's grandchildren followed in his wake. Brody locked eyes with a dark-haired preschooler about his own age, holding the hand of Seth's oldest daughter, Amelia.

Agnes smoothed her floral-patterned skirt. "Anytime your mom is busy or out of town this summer, you give me a call, Jaxon." She smiled at his son. "I'd love to spend the day with this young man."

"I appreciate your offer, but I couldn't—"

She flitted her hand. "No trouble, it's my pleasure. I have to live vicariously." Her eyes cut to Darcy. "No grandchildren of my own." Her gaze shot to him. "Yet."

Darcy went crimson.

Harold clasped Jax's hand. "I need to speak with the organist before service begins. But I hope we'll see more of you in the future."

Darcy gnashed her teeth. But proper PK that she was, she held it together.

"How about I take Brody to children's church?" Agnes motioned toward Amelia's son, who was heading to the education wing. "Would you like to meet my friend Patrick Scott, Brody?"

Brody glowered.

Jax didn't relish a scene in front of the entire congregation. "Maybe I ought to keep Brody with me." His son looked up at his name. "He doesn't like strangers."

Agnes cocked her head. "There'll be cookies, Brody."

Brody held up his arms, and Agnes picked him up.

Jax flushed. The only stranger Brody didn't care for was his own father. Maybe he should take up baking. If only it were that simple in righting the wrong between him and his son.

Agnes whisked Brody away. And Jax decided to keep his distance from Darcy. The resident PK always took the closest pew to the front, so he settled into an empty pew a few rows back, across the aisle.

Where were his parents? He rubbernecked during the prelude, scanning the foyer. Where were Anna and Ryan? Charlie and Evy? Reinforcements of any kind?

But it was Ryan's siblings who rescued him from sitting out the service by himself. In the quirky, if endearing, Southern definition of family—blood relations or not—the Savages welcomed him.

Luke slid into the pew beside Jax. "Hey, man."

"You're not sitting here alone?" Ryan's bubbly youngest sister, Tessa, had grown up in Jax's absence.

"We can't have that, can we?" Justine the

Klutz—Mom's words, not his—fell over his feet into the pew.

He couldn't help noticing that their other brother, Ethan, plopped beside Darcy. And she smiled at him. Irritated, Jax scowled. Only the preacher's family was supposed to sit there.

As Ethan Savage and Darcy continued to chat it up, other old friends stopped by to greet Jax, surprising him.

He'd been gone a long time. Yet perhaps that was the truest measure of good friends—the ability to take right up again, no matter how long the time between conversations. Kind of like him and Darcy.

Who was still talking a blue streak to Ethan Savage. Using her hands like she did when she was excited.

In a deliberate act of self-discipline—his Green Beret training—Jax fastened his eyes on the podium. Refusing to track what Darcy was doing across the aisle.

At the last possible moment, his parents, Charlie and Evy slid into the pew in front of Jax. Something about a leak in the bathroom, his mom murmured. Anna and Ryan had nursery duty. The congregation rose for the first hymn.

His self-control cracking, Jax glanced over to find Darcy elbowing Ethan in the ribs as they shared a hymnal. Jax didn't feel like singing.

The sermon proved easier. Harold Parks knew

how to hold the congregation's attention. Jax kept his face forward and concentrated hard on being an attentive listener.

"Our text this morning is from John 8:36." Reverend Parks smiled before reading the passage. "So if the Son sets you free, you will be free indeed."

Freedom, a great concept in the abstract. In Jax's case, impossible. He shifted on the wooden pew. What he wouldn't give to lose the heavy stone crushing his heart since Adrienne died.

The pastor paused, his gaze falling briefly on each member of his flock. Was it Jax's imagination or did it linger slightly longer on him?

"He whom the Son sets free is free indeed." Harold's eyes darted to the front pew. "Reminds me of a young girl who loved to swing."

Jax saw Darcy recoil, as if she'd taken a blow to the head. But she recovered quickly, donning the stiff PK shield she often wore.

The swing to which Reverend Parks referred had hung empty and forlorn as long as Jax had known her. He wasn't acquainted with the swing-loving side of Darcy her father so fondly recalled. And judging by her hunched shoulders, it wasn't a memory Darcy was fond of recalling.

She loved her parents. Over the years, she'd sacrificed a lot to please them. To be the perfect PK. But a disconnect existed between Darcy and her father. Then came an unsettling thought. Kind of like the breach between Jax and his son.

Jax glanced at his mother. From the pursing of her lips, he knew she'd noticed Darcy's reaction, too. The reverend was a good, caring man. But Darcy would've have gotten more personal attention if she'd been any other child in his congregation rather than his own.

Had the swing-loving Darcy disappeared about the same time she took to her tree house roost? Peering out at the world and the Pruitts' backyard with those big, blue-green eyes of hers?

To her credit, Gail Pruitt had done something about it. Going out of her way to include the little preacher's kid in the escapades of her own rampaging brood.

In their yard, Darcy was never the PK. She was just Darcy. With her in-your-face, larger than life dreams.

The reverend went on to relate his child's nearly airborne freedom on the swing. The exhilaration on her face. How he'd shared in her delight and joy. As their Heavenly Father delighted in His children's joy. A joy most perfectly found within Himself.

"Whatever you face today, dear friends, whatever weighs you down, keeping you chained in misery and dread, let God be your burden-bearer. I beg you to find true rest and peace in Him."

Those words forced Jax to examine his paltry efforts outside of God's strength thus far. The pastor made it sound so easy. To stop striving. To stop working toward making your own peace. But that went against the grain of everything Jax was—as a firstborn, as a Green Beret, as a painfully wounded man.

Harold Parks gripped the sides of the podium. "And once we allow God to be our burden-bearer, each of us must be brave enough to answer God's further call on our lives. To become a burden-sharer with one another."

Like Darcy was trying to help Jax with Brody.

As for the weight of his muddled guilt over Adrienne? He bowed his head as the reverend closed in prayer.

In his heart, Jax believed the guilt to be a cross he'd have to bear alone. And suddenly, home felt farther out of his reach than he'd supposed. Farther than when they'd lowered Adrienne's casket into the frozen Utah ground.

That afternoon, Darcy stared at the hand-carved initials on the tree house railing. They were weathered and barely visible now... She ran her finger over the indentions, tracing the C and the P. Colin Parks.

She'd been five when she overheard a couple of ladies discussing the tragic loss of her father's first family. Her mother hadn't wanted to answer the questions bursting out of Darcy's small chest.

And still processing that she wasn't her father's only child, she'd used the railing on the bottom platform as a monkey bar. Upside down that same day, she'd spotted the carving.

Her father—their father—had carved his son's initials into the wood. She'd realized then that the tree house had been built for Colin, not her. And that it—like their father's heart—belonged to her dead little half brother.

Closing her eyes, Darcy leaned against the railing. Birds chirped in the canopy overhead. A briny sea breeze floated past her nostrils.

Was it Darcy her father had pushed in the swing? Or did he visualize his small son, alive in its pendulum motion? Either way, she'd never gotten in the swing again.

It'd been strange to hear her father talk in his sermon about what used to be their cherished time together. Disconcerting. He was always careful not to use her or Mom as an object lesson. Unless it was a good memory. As apparently, the swing was for him. Her, too, until…

Pressure built in her chest. She gazed at what constituted her world. The screened porch where on Sunday afternoons her father took a much-needed nap. The deck of the Pruitt house next door. The street out front, where she'd lived her entire life…

All at once, she couldn't breathe. And she knew

she needed to escape, at least for a while. From the pressures, the expectations, the loneliness.

Without bothering to change clothes, she got into her car. The driveway next door was packed with vehicles. Gail Pruitt and Evy would've done it up right for Sunday family lunch. The choked feeling inside Darcy mounted.

Minutes later, she pulled into the parking lot of Kiptohanock Kayaking. Summer employee Chas and their clients would arrive later for the Sunday afternoon excursion. But now was her chance.

Her skirt swirled as she hurried around the corner of the building, keys in hand. She would unlock the storage building. Retrieve her personal kayak and paddle.

Darcy's footfalls crunched across the sandy soil. There was nothing on earth like that first moment as the kayak glided out onto the water. The serenity, the calm, the absolute stillness of reaching the marsh and—

She stuttered to a halt as Jax emerged, PFD in hand, from the outbuilding. *Why, God?* When all she'd wanted...

Catching sight of her, he grinned. "Long time no see, Parks."

"What are you doing here, Jax?"

This was her time. Her place. Her shop— Actually, it wasn't. Her heart wrenched.

He inclined his head. "Thought I'd get in some R & R on a lazy Sunday afternoon."

"Where is your son?" The words spit out of her mouth in a staccato punch.

Jax's eyes narrowed. "Napping at Mom's," he said. "Kind of unusual for him, Brody being such a big boy. Almost three, you know."

"I wanted to do a short paddle. If that's okay with you?" She lifted her chin, galled that she had to ask the new owner's permission for something she did every Sunday afternoon.

"Be my guest." His arm swept toward the dock. "Thought I'd do the same."

She moistened her bottom lip. "I'll come another—"

"The water's big enough for the two of us, Darce."

"Is it, Jax?" She tilted her head. "Is it really?"

"The water. The town. The Shore. I reckon they are."

"Virginia. America. The world." Darcy threw out her hand. "I'm not so sure, Jax."

A speculative look entered his eyes. A look that, in her vast, personal experience with Jaxon Pruitt, usually boded no good. At least for her.

"I'm not unaware of the conspiracy that has put this summer into motion, Darce."

"Conspiracy?"

"Shirley, the shop, the Keys…"

Kicking off her flip-flops, Darcy widened her stance on the sand.

"This afternoon. This spot. You and me." He

quirked his eyebrows. "It was my dad who suggested I take advantage of Brody's nap, and come here for a little paddle. Never saw that coming. Not from him."

Her mouth tightened. "We've been played."

"Again."

She turned to go. "I'll leave you to it and—"

"How about we give 'em something to talk about, Darce? Let 'em think they succeeded."

"What're you suggesting?"

Jax let one shoulder rise and fall. "Let's do one better. Let's get out the tandem kayak."

Her eyes widened. "Go together for a paddle? In the same boat?"

A smile tweaked his lips. "Why not? Because the way I see it, we're already in the same boat. The boat they've maneuvered us into. Maybe then they'll let us alone. What do you say?"

"I don't think it's a good idea."

For many reasons. Most of which she'd never have the courage to share with Jax Pruitt. Standing there, the sunshine highlighting the gold strands in his brown hair. Looking way too good. Way too everything.

"Despite, and I quote, 'I wouldn't get on board with you, Jaxon Pruitt, if the ship was sinking and you were the last lifeboat' end quote. I dare you, Darcy Parks."

She tapped her bare foot. He wasn't going to let this go. And she'd never been one to shy away from a challenge. Especially one issued by her arch nemesis Jaxon I'm-So-Handsome Pruitt.

"Fine." She poked out her lips.

As he ducked his head to enter the storage building, she didn't miss the gleam of pure satisfaction in Jax's gaze. He returned, dragging the tandem kayak. His eyes landed on the hem of her skirt, brushing against her kneecaps. And she glimpsed not only satisfaction, but something else. Appreciation?

"Looking good, summer girl."

With a life jacket threaded over his arm, he tucked his head, rotated his hips and his shoulders, doing that swagger thing he did. "I wouldn't have changed into cargo shorts if I'd realized Sunday paddles had a dress code."

Her skin probably glowing as red as a firecracker, she took the PFD from him. "I'll help you drag the boat to the dock."

"I got this, Darce." He swished his hand, reminding her of their swashbuckling childhood. "Nothing for your pretty red head to worry about."

She glared. "I'm not a—" Wait. Had he called her pretty?

Darcy was so stunned, she didn't put up any resistance when he carefully handed her into the kayak. And she was too discombobulated to protest when she found herself seated in the stern, not the bow.

She tucked her skirt around her legs. She didn't

usually wear a skirt on a paddle, but her mind had been elsewhere this afternoon. On things she'd spent a lifetime avoiding. She surveyed the broad, muscled shoulders of the man seated in front of her. Things including him.

His corded forearms sliced the paddle through the blue-green waters. She matched her stroke to his. They glided along the inlet.

Leaving the busy harbor, they entered a narrow tidal creek, not far from the Duer Inn. With an upsweep of its wings, a great blue heron lifted off from the salt marsh.

Jax stopped paddling, resting his paddle across his lap. They sat in silence for a few moments, savoring the sights, sounds and smells of their Eastern Shore world.

"So did we pass the test, Darce?" He didn't turn around.

Darcy preferred not to have to face him. Easier to gather her thoughts. The grown-up Jax disturbed her on a profound level.

She played obtuse. "What test?"

"The kayak test. I think we work well together, don't you?"

Jax Pruitt didn't really want to know what she thought. She bit her lip, lest her words betray her.

"The test of mutual trust." He angled to glance back at her. "We make a good team, Darce."

She inhaled sharply. "What are you playing at, Jax? What do you want from me?"

His eyes darkened. "Darcy…"

"I learned the hard way never to trust you." She flung out her hand, dislodging her paddle. She made a quick grab for it, nearly losing it overboard. "There is no happily-ever-paddle when it comes to us. You made your choice a long time ago. You just need to suck it up and deal."

He flinched.

Runner-up Darcy. Second choice to the army. Now, a dead wife? She would walk the plank before she was anybody's consolation prize.

"Spent any time on that swing lately, Darce?" His voice was a dangerous purr.

Darcy went cold, then hot. "Stop…" She shuddered. "Just stop, Jax…"

Anger stitched his mouth into a flat line. His hands clenched around the paddle shaft. "Till summer's end. I get it, Darcy."

She gripped her own paddle. "I'm going home."

Using the blade as a rudder, she made a valiant but futile attempt to rotate the kayak. Huffing with exertion, she blew an errant lock of hair out of her eyes, straining.

Jax watched, letting her struggle for a second, before he dipped his blade in the water, too. With his help, the craft turned.

Back at the dock, she scrambled out of the kayak. Almost capsizing, he grabbed the sides to steady himself. And past caring about getting wet, she plowed through the water. Her skirt plastered around her legs, the hem dragged against her knees.

She stalked past her abandoned flip-flops, not bothering to retrieve them. And then she ran as if her life depended on it. She should've stayed away. Why couldn't she just stay away? Choking back sobs, she sprinted toward her SUV, not caring who saw her.

Because somehow her life, her sanity, her plans, her dreams, depended on staying as far away from Jax as she could.

Chapter Eight

Jax had a hard time falling asleep that night. And a harder time rising the next morning. What Reverend Parks said about freedom had gone around and around in his head. As did the look on Darcy's face when she'd stormed out of the kayak.

He didn't know why he'd brought up the kayak test. He was ashamed of bringing up the swing. No excuses. He'd known exactly what he was doing in pushing her buttons.

She didn't realize it, but he was doing her a favor in pushing her away.

He was surprised to find Brody still in bed. His son usually woke with the dawn, which meant Jax did, too. But today was Monday, and the business was closed. So there was no big urgency to get out the door.

After much prodding, Brody responded, but his eyes were dull and shadowed. His hair sleep-tousled, he sat on the edge of the bed and watched Jax remove clothes from the bureau.

Jax laid the shirt and pants beside his son. "Time to get dressed, Brody."

Brody slumped, making no move toward the clothes. Jax frowned. It wasn't like him to be lethargic.

"Need help, buddy?"

Brody nodded. Again, not the norm from Mr. Me Do.

Jax helped him slip out of his gym shorts and Captain America T-shirt. Brody shivered, although the temperature outside already hovered around eighty degrees.

When Jax eased the blue T-shirt over his head, Brody allowed him to lift his arm and insert it through the sleeve. He felt warm to the touch, but Jax reasoned he had been snugly wrapped in his bedcovers.

Had Brody somehow gotten overheated on the Big Wheel at Grandpa's yesterday? Jax had made sure he was properly protected with sunscreen and bug spray. Had he drunk enough water? Maybe he was dehydrated.

"Let's get breakfast, Brode."

Without a word, Brody slipped off the mattress and plodded after Jax toward the kitchen. The little boy stopped at the base of his booster seat, staring at it as one might contemplate Everest.

Brody held up his arms.

Heart hammering, Jax lifted him and placed him in the seat. His son radiated heat and also a faint clamminess.

This wasn't like Brody. Not at all. Darcy held him. His grandmother and Agnes Parks, too. But never Jax. Something wasn't right.

He poured cereal into a bowl. As if his neck suddenly was unable to bear the weight, Brody laid his head on the table.

Jax came around the island to his son. "What's wrong, Brody?"

Listless, the little boy closed his eyes. "No hungwy," he whispered. His little lips were chapped.

The day Brody Pruitt wasn't hungry...

Jax laid his palm on Brody's forehead. "Does your stomach hurt?"

Was it his imagination, or was Brody warmer than he'd been a few minutes ago, getting dressed?

"Does your head hurt?"

A single tear welled in Brody's eye. Jax watched its silent trek down the length of Brody's cheek. His heart caught in his throat.

"Son? Talk to me. Please."

Raising his head, Brody promptly vomited all over himself and burst into tears.

The child—who'd never even cried when his mother died—sobbed in Jax's arms.

Fear lanced Jax's heart. His too-stoic little boy was sick. Very sick.

"I'm here, Brody. Daddy's here."

Quick as he could, Jax got Brody cleaned up and carried him out to the truck. He sped down Seaside Road, glad his by-the-book deputy sheriff brother wasn't around. But one look at his kid and Brody's marshmallow Uncle Charlie would've probably hit the siren and given them a police escort.

Jax gripped the wheel, darting a look in the rearview mirror. "Hang in there, buddy." Brody's head lolled against the seat.

"Brody?" His pulse lurched. "Answer Daddy, please."

He grunted, momentarily reassuring Jax.

Jax bypassed Kiptohanock and headed north on Highway 13. When he was a boy, Kiptohanock had had its own general practitioner, but not anymore.

Belatedly, he realized he should've called ahead to the doctor's office. Jax white-knuckled the wheel, as scared as he'd ever been on his worst mission.

What was he doing, trying to be somebody's dad? He didn't know anything about sick kids. He barreled to a stop in the medical office parking lot. He grabbed Brody and ran.

Jax caught sight of himself in the glass door. An expression on his face he recognized from combat missions—grim, determined, don't-get-in-my-way. The nurse took one look at him and hustled them through the waiting area to an examination room. An antiseptic smell assaulted his nostrils.

The nurse was a friend of his mother's. "Lay him on the table."

But when Jax did so, his son whimpered and held on to his hand.

"I'm right here, Brody." Jax set his jaw. "I'm not going anywhere." His boy looked so tiny and pale on the white paper sheet.

He swallowed. Darcy was right. Despite being almost "thwee," Brody was still a baby. His baby.

The nurse adjusted the stethoscope around her neck and reached for Brody, who let out a hoarse cry of fear.

Sinking onto the crinkling paper, Jax gathered him in his arms. Brody clung to him.

"No shot..." The child quivered against him. "No shot."

He rubbed small circles on Brody's back. "The nurse is going to help you feel better, son." He glared at her. "You *are* going to make him feel better, right?"

The nurse's face softened. "We're sure going to try. I need to get his vitals and take his temperature first, though."

Jax nodded. But when he began peeling him off his chest, Brody protested. Loudly.

If he required an injection... Jax's gut clenched. Brody would fight them, as he would have at his age. Jax would have to hold Brody down, and he'd hate him even more. But if that's what it took to make Brody well...

Jax answered the nurse's preliminary questions as best he could. An elderly man in a white coat entered the room. Brody writhed in Jax's arms as the doctor checked the boy's ears, nose and throat.

The doctor appeared unruffled by the struggle. "Have you given him anything for the fever?"

Jax felt like he'd gone ten rounds with a terrorist. And lost. He was a terrible father. He should've had a first aid kit stocked at home.

"No." He pinched his lips together. "I didn't know what to do."

The doc patted Brody's head. Brody howled like a crazed thing.

"You did the right thing in bringing him here. His ears and throat look fine. I think it's the summer virus that's been going around. A lot of children on the Shore are sick with it. Let's get the fever down."

Jax sagged in relief. "He's going to be okay?"

"Keep him on plenty of fluids. It should pass within twenty-four to forty-eight hours. If not, bring him back." The doctor smiled, rearranging the wrinkles on his face. "You've got quite the little warrior here."

His arms tightened around his son. Yes, he did. "So no shots?"

"Not unless you really want one." The doctor's lips curved. "The virus just needs to run its course."

"Thank you so much, Doctor." Jax bent his mouth toward Brody's ear. "No shots today, son."

In a remarkable, immediate transformation, Brody gathered his dignity about himself. The doctor left final instructions.

Brody gave the nurse, holding a vial of pink liquid, a steely-eyed scowl. "No!"

She arched her eyebrow. "No medicine, no lollipop."

"Bribery?" Jax gaped. "Seriously?"

She shrugged. "Sometimes you just gotta do what you gotta do."

Brody's eyes narrowed, but like a baby bird, he leaned forward, lips parted. The noxious liquid went down the hatch. He made a face.

"Dude." Jax ruffled Brody's hair. "That was brave, man."

Brody presented his outstretched palm to the nurse. Jax's jaw dropped. Obviously at some point Brody had done this before.

"Grape or cherry?" The nurse pulled open a drawer. "And Jax, please give my regards to your mom."

After checking out, it was with no small measure of personal triumph that Jax carried Brody from the office. The fever reducer was already taking effect. A grape lollipop clenched between his lips, Brody rode in Jax's arms, the conquering hero.

Only a virus? Thank God it hadn't been anything more serious. But he quailed at the prospect of a dozen more years of childhood illnesses. Tucking Brody into his seat, Jax exhaled.

The nurse had given him enough fever reducer samples to avoid a detour to the pharmacy. At home, he gave Brody a few sips of an electrolyte drink. After waiting to make sure he kept that down, he gave him more.

Brody refused to return to his bed, preferring to watch television. Which was fine by Jax. Settling on the couch with the remote, he and Brody watched the morning lineup of kid shows.

Midway during the first one, Brody crawled onto his lap. Jax's breath hitched. He was sorry Brody wasn't feeling well, but he'd take what Brody offered while he could. By the second animated children's show, his own weariness started to overtake him.

Keeping Brody tucked under his arm, he inched to the corner of the couch. Stretching out his legs, Jax leaned his head on the armrest. Brody's eyelids drooped, as worn out as Jax by the morning's trauma.

Touching Brody's forehead, Jax was relieved to find his skin cooler. There were still a few more hours until the next dose, but the medicine was doing its job. Brody's eyes closed, his eyelashes fanning his cheeks.

When he shifted, Jax opened his arms. And to his surprise, Brody planted himself facedown on

Jax's chest, his little forehead resting against the exposed skin above Jax's T-shirt. The lump in Jax's throat grew.

Careful not to wake the sleeping Cubby Bear, Jax placed his hands on Brody's back, and found his breaths deep and even. And an immense gratitude welled within Jax. For his son. For home. For a future together.

Tears pricked his eyes. He'd lie here all day if that's what it took to make Brody feel comfortable. Jax had nowhere to go, and no place he'd rather be than on this sofa with his son in his arms.

Something within him—a feeling he'd not realized he was capable of—relished that he could give Brody what he needed most. And for the moment, it was enough.

Darcy didn't think anything of it when she pulled up to the empty outfitter shop on Tuesday. She hadn't spoken to Jax since Sunday afternoon. She'd talked her parents into spending Monday at the Ocean City boardwalk.

She'd needed the time away from everything reminding her of Jax. She needed time to regroup. To school her emotions into the place they belonged. She meant it this time.

After today—with some artful planning—their paths never need cross at work again. Darcy unlocked the store. The path not taken. A path not meant to be. At least, not for her.

She was relieved not to have to face Jax first thing, but he'd be in later to go over the accounts. With restless energy, she went outside, set on taking each of the paddle joints apart. Using a bottle-brush, she cleaned the throat of the blade where it tapered to the shaft. Once it was thoroughly scoured, she leaned each paddle against the outbuilding to dry.

It was best to keep busy. To leave no time for imagination. Or dream of something doomed from the start.

By the time she finished, her shoulders ached. Savannah had arrived for the morning expedition, gone out and come back. The sun arced high overhead.

Stretching her tight muscles, Darcy gazed over the harbor, taking an unconscious inventory of the prevailing wind and chop of the water, as any born here would.

And then, because her thoughts inevitably drifted to Jax… She glanced at her cell. He should've been here by now.

Her mouth thinned. So much for his so-called desire to tackle the books this morning. Was this what his commitment to the business meant?

This was so…so Jax. So typical of his attitude to life. To everything. To her.

She marched toward the storefront, her flip-flops clomping. From the beginning, this had been a bad idea. She should've been the new owner, not someone as unreliable as him.

At the cash register, Savannah was ringing up a customer's purchases. Nearby Ozzie was booking a sunset excursion for a family. On the laptop, Darcy checked email and then voice mail. No message. She pried her cell out of her jeans short's pocket again. Nothing.

Darcy fumed. She'd had about all she was going to take from Jaxon Pruitt. She hit his speed dial and clamped the phone to her ear.

Waiting, she tapped her foot on the linoleum as it rang. And rang. Why wasn't he picking up? Unless he was avoiding her calls. Which was so irresponsible. So…

She'd tell him a thing or two. Or three before she was done. And when she was finished with him, he'd wish he'd never—

"Hello?" She gripped the phone. "Jaxon?" She gnashed her teeth. "Jaxon Pruitt? Answer me."

"Me Bwody Pwoo-it. Hey, Dawcy."

Her stomach jerked. "Brody?" Why was he answering Jax's phone? "Brody, talk to me, baby."

"Me not baby," he growled.

"Of course you're not a baby, sweetheart," she backpedaled. "I meant… Can I talk to your daddy?"

"No, Dawcy. He sick."

Her mouth went dry. "Your daddy's sick? Where are you, sweetheart?"

What had happened? Were they stranded on the side of the road somewhere? After what happened to Anna—

"Home, Dawcy."

"Okay, Brody. You stay right where you are."

Duh. Where would he go? He was two years old.

"Me hungwy, Dawcy. He sick."

"I'll be there as quick as I can, honey. Darcy's coming."

"'Kay." *Click.*

She stared at the cell in her hand. A little man of few words. She swallowed, hard. Apples never did fall far from trees.

Leaving Ozzie and Savannah to manage things, she threw herself into the SUV and raced the engine. How long had Jax been sick? What was wrong with him? Should she have dialed 911?

Why hadn't Jax called her? Though perhaps he'd been unable to call anyone. Racing over the bridge out of town, she pressed harder on the accelerator.

Green rows of corn flew past on either side of the road. Isolated white farmhouses and woodland blurred. The turnoff to the Duer Inn. Past the Savage garden center...

Wrenching the wheel, she pulled into Jaxon's long driveway. And skidded to a stop, the tires spraying shell. Jumping out, she ran toward the porch, leaving the car door open, the alarm dinging in her wake.

His brown head visible through the bay window, Brody waved. His face broke into a smile. She fumbled for the key Shirley had given her a long time ago. And was glad she'd forgotten to turn it over to Jax when he took occupancy of the house.

The door squeaked as she poked her head around the frame. In a flash, Brody appeared, his arms clasping her knees.

"Hey, Dawcy."

She hugged his small body. "Are you okay? Where's your daddy?"

Brody jabbed his thumb in the direction of the living room. Taking his hand, she ventured further inside, but the living room was empty. Sounds of retching traveled down the staircase from the bathroom. She winced.

"Me sick."

She inspected his features. "You're sick, too?"

Brody shook his head. "No mow."

She spotted a receipt from the pediatrician's office on the kitchen island. "You were sick…" she examined the date "…yesterday. How long has Daddy been sick?"

Brody climbed onto a stool. "Me hungwy, Dawcy."

Crumbs from an empty packet of cookies dotted the countertop. A half-eaten banana and a juice pack lay near the sink. Brody had been trolling for food he could reach.

A toilet flushed, and Jax staggered down the stairs, only to come to an abrupt standstill at the bottom.

"Wh-what are you doing here?" His voice gravelly, he darted his eyes to his son. "Is Brody okay?"

Her lips pursed. "Brody seems to be fine. You, however..."

Clad in sweatpants, he crossed his arms around the seen-better-days army T-shirt. The khaki green matched the greenish cast around his mouth.

His feet were bare. She averted her gaze. Sick or well, Jaxon made her pulse thrum.

Jax ran his hand through his disheveled hair, making it worse. "Why are you here?"

"Why are you such a stubborn idiot?" As always, anger was a far safer emotion when dealing with Jax. "Why didn't you call your mom? You need help."

He lifted his chin, covered with two days' worth of scruff. "I do not need help. I took care of Brody myself. I'm fine."

"You are not fine." She gestured. "Just look at you. You can barely stand."

As if to illustrate her point, he leaned against the wall. Usually the leaning annoyed her. Today, because of his illness, she was willing to give him the benefit of the doubt.

"I'm fine. We're fine. I don't need—"

"You've been perfectly clear about what you don't need." She turned her back on him, facing Brody. "Your son is hungry, and I intend to feed him."

"I peeled a banana for him earlier... Before..." He gave a strangled sound.

Hand over mouth, Jax bolted toward the staircase.

"You're fine," she called. "Sure you are."

Despite the ninety-degree temps outside, she heated chicken noodle soup on the oven range. "Just the thing, Brody, when you've been feeling under the weather."

She was ladling soup into a bowl when Jax emerged once more. He looked like death warmed over.

On his face, humiliation warred with a sheepish gratitude. "I guess I might need to lie down for a few minutes, if you don't mind."

Leaving Brody to slurp the soup, she moved toward Jax. He backed away.

"I don't want you to get sick, too. Doc says it's a twenty-four-hour bug. I probably got it from Brody."

Brody banged his foot against the island. "Me not a bug, Daddy." He laughed.

She and Jax gasped simultaneously.

"Did he just call me...?" Jax looked away, but not before she'd spotted the welling in his eyes.

"I told you it would be okay between you guys." She blinked back her own tears. "That you had to give him time."

He nodded, unable to speak for the emotion cresting across his face. He swayed.

She frowned. "Chas can't do the sunset excursion today. But I'm staying till then. Whether you like it or not."

"I—I... Okay."

Did he feel as miserable as he looked?

She motioned to the upper story. "You need to go to bed."

He shook his head. "I'd rather camp out on the couch." He dropped his eyes. "That way I can enjoy the two of you." His lashes flicked upward, his eyes meeting hers.

Darcy's pulse skittered like a kayak skimming the waves of the sea.

But it wouldn't do to appear too pleased. Not good for her heart. Or Jaxon's overlarge ego. But she was pleased. Ridiculously so. That he trusted her with his son. And that he wanted to be with her.

She tried for stern. "As long as you promise to rest." She folded her arms. "One child on my hands is enough. I don't need two."

He sank onto the sofa. "Deal."

She suspected he'd sat down just before he would've fallen. Sitting upright, he closed his eyes.

Darcy retrieved a pillow from his bedroom upstairs. "Lie back. You'll rest better." She pulled at him.

Without protest, he laid his head on the pillow and stretched out. She fanned a quilt over him.

"Thank you, Darce," he whispered. "You're the best friend ever."

She examined Brody. She hoped as much soup had made it into his mouth as stained his shirt. "You, young man, are in desperate need of a bath."

His sneer told her what he thought of her suggestion.

"Your daddy is sick, and I'm guessing you missed your bath last night." She cocked her head. "You don't want Daddy worrying, do you? We need to take care of him."

Brody perked up. "Me take cawc Daddy."

She cut her eyes to Jax on the sofa. His eyes were closed, but a faint smile etched his lips.

Darcy held out her hand to Brody. "I know you'll take care of your daddy. Because you're such a good, big boy."

Brody jumped off the stool with a leap that would've made a paratrooper proud. "Me big."

Her eyes watered. "Yes, you are." Such a sweet, big boy. A chip off the old block.

Walking to the couch, Brody laid his small hand across Jax's forehead. Probably something his father had done yesterday with him.

Brody shook his head. "Not hot. Not cowd."

"Just right." Jax opened one eye and winked

at Darcy. "What I've been telling you, Darce, for years."

"Your ego seems no worse for wear." She rolled her eyes. "Good to know you're on the mend, Goldilocks."

Brody patted his father's cheek. "Wuv you, Daddy."

Jax's eyes misted. "I—I love you, too, son."

Her heart thumped against her rib cage. "Come on, Brody." She tugged his hand. "Let's get that bath."

Jax caught her sleeve. "Thanks, Darcy." He gulped. "For everything."

He turned his face toward the cushion. And she left him to his unaccustomed emotion. She loved how tough Mr. Green Beret became emotional gelatin with his son. Her own nerve endings felt raw and exposed when it came to both Pruitts, man and boy.

And despite losing the business, she was suddenly glad, very glad, that Jaxon Pruitt had come home to Kiptohanock.

Chapter Nine

Darcy had gotten less wet rolling the kayak than she did giving Brody a bath. And every time he splashed her, he dissolved into stomach-clutching guffaws.

Not a word she normally used. But yes, guffaws. Brody believed himself hysterically funny. She bit back a smile. He kind of was.

Toweling him off, she reflected that he was a far different child than the too solemn boy she'd met only a few weeks ago. Something had happened between him and Jax during this bout of illness. Something had dissolved the barricades around Brody's heart and convinced him to trust his father.

His bare feet padded into his bedroom. Towel around his waist, he pulled Spider-Man underwear out of a drawer. "Me do." He gave her a pointed look.

Not a battle she wanted to fight.

"Knock yourself out, Brode." She halted in the doorway. "You know that's just an expression, right?"

"What's 'spression, Dawcy?"

"Something people say." She fluttered her hand. "Just get dressed, and don't do anything crazy."

He let out a belly laugh. Which coming out of his almost-three-year-old mouth sounded slightly ominous. "Me go cwazy, Dawcy." He arched his eyebrows. "Awgh!" Like some long-ago-buccaneer.

Pondering the need to call in reinforcements— like her mom—she wheeled around and ran smack into Jax's muscled chest. She bounced into the wall.

"Sorry." He stepped away.

"I didn't know you were—"

"I thought you heard—" His brow furrowed.

She moistened her lips. "You're supposed to be resting."

His face turned wistful. "Y'all were having so much fun, I didn't want to miss anything."

Fun? Her gaze darted from her drenched shirt to her wet feet. She'd ditched the flip-flops after the first attempt to wrangle Brody into the tub.

She let out a laugh. "Yeah, it was fun." Truth be told, it had been.

And sick or not, Jaxon exuded a raw, masculine charisma. Standing this close to him had her pulse zinging. His son already possessed that kind of charm in spades. She watched Brody wrestle a T-shirt over his head. Shore girls would be in big trouble in about a dozen years.

"You should be lying down."

Rolling his tongue in his cheek, Jax gave her a two-fingered salute. "Yes, ma'am."

Blowing a small breath between her lips, she slunk past him. Charm out the wazoo. She should know better than to let him get under her skin and inside her heart.

Her eyes went wide, and she stopped in her tracks. Is that what she'd—

This time, Jax ran into her back, and bounced. "Sorry. I didn't mean to—"

"I thought you were—" She made a sweeping motion. "Just lie down, Jax."

Without arguing, he turned on his heel and went downstairs again.

Brody apparently believed in accessorizing his underwear. He came out wearing a Spider-Man shirt and pants, looking incredibly adorable. One day he'd be as handsome as…

Idle hands led to idle thoughts. Darcy decided to give the kitchen a thorough overhaul. Afterward, she set the bathroom to rights.

And Jax lay on the sofa, watching her with that half-lidded stare of his. But eventually, he drifted off into a peaceful sleep. Finger on her lips, she hushed Brody and gave him a snack.

Still in recovery himself, in the midst of playing with his trucks, Brody fell asleep in front of the couch.

Darcy took advantage of the lull to tackle his room. On the bedside table, she discovered a framed photograph of Jax and a woman holding infant Brody. Sinking onto the mattress, Darcy studied the features of the woman who'd borne Brody and captured Jax's heart.

Even in combat fatigues, Adrienne Maserelli was beautiful. She'd retained her maiden name, a sore spot with Jax's father, Darcy had heard. In the picture, intelligence shone out of Adrienne's face. Of a Mediterranean heritage, she possessed an exotic beauty with her sloe eyes, high cheekbones and dark hair.

She'd been an ambitious, highly accomplished and sophisticated soldier in her own right. Unlike Darcy, whose skill set amounted to navigating a plastic boat through the water. Adrienne and Jax had made a striking couple. Darcy's gut twisted.

"Why is it you've never asked about Adrienne?" Jax lounged against the doorway of Brody's room.

"Sorry." Hands shaking, Darcy set the frame on the nightstand. "I didn't mean to be nosy."

He cocked his head. "The photograph was taken on one of our few good days together as a family."

She wasn't sure how to respond to that, so she stayed silent.

"After Adrienne died, Mom put together a photo album for Brody."

Unfolding, Jax moved toward the built-in bookcase and pulled out a leather-bound album. "He doesn't remember his mother. He was only a year old when she was killed, and she's been gone just as long. These photos are all he'll ever have of her."

Carrying the book, Jax sat down on the mattress. The last thing Darcy wanted was to watch him grieve over his dead wife, so she stepped backward. "I better check—"

"Don't go. Please." Jax touched her arm. "He's still asleep. There aren't many people with whom I can talk about Adrienne."

Wringing her hands, Darcy bit her lip. Jax wanted to talk to her about his wife? Oh, joy.

But at the pain in his dark eyes, she gave up thinking about herself. She couldn't leave him hurting this way.

So she pulled a chair from the desk and set it across from Jax. Maintaining as much distance as possible, for her sake, if not for his.

He opened the album. "Adrienne and I…" He flipped a page. "We were complicated."

That was not what Darcy expected.

"Adrienne was the most competitive person I'd ever met." He gave Darcy a wry grin. "Which considering who I am, says a lot."

A smile tugged at her lips. "The most competitive person *I've* ever met."

"But it was more than that. Adrienne and I were like fire and ice."

Darcy fidgeted.

"After we were married, I realized those two elements aren't a good combination. Either fire melts ice or ice douses fire."

She knotted her hands in her lap.

"We brought out the worst in each other. Staying together meant one of us was in danger of being extinguished. We had nothing in common, except the army."

"You had Brody in common," she whispered.

His laugh was tinged with disillusionment. "You'd think so, wouldn't you? But Adrienne wasn't happy when she discovered she was pregnant. A child didn't fit into her career plans."

Darcy's chin lifted. "But Brody is wonderful."

Tenderness softened the rugged planes of Jax's face. "Yeah, he is." Jax swallowed. "And in her own way, she loved him."

"What does that mean, Jax?"

"Adrienne came from a prominent family in Salt Lake City. She spent her entire adult life trying to prove them wrong when they disagreed about her joining the military, instead of the family firm. Deployment was one way up the ranks."

That hit a little too close to home, and Darcy took a breath. "So she wasn't around a lot."

"Me, either. Dual deployments are a reality for many military couples. But when there are children involved…"

"It becomes harder."

Jax closed the album. "The first ten months of Brody's life we argued constantly. Something I hope he won't remember. She wanted me to give up my career. I wanted her to opt out of deployment. Neither of us would give an inch."

"Where was Brody when you both deployed?"

"Mom came once. A military friend's wife took care of him, too. Adrienne and I had a major blowout right before she shipped out the last time." Anguish rippled across Jax's features. "She informed me that when she returned she was filing for divorce. And I could try single-parenting for a change. See how I liked it."

"Oh, Jax. What did you do?"

"I was stunned." He scrubbed his hand over his face. "But there wasn't much I could do. I was flying out on my own mission. I planned to talk more when we both returned. When we were both calmer." He sighed. "So much for my plans, huh?"

Her heart physically ached from the hurt he must've felt. The betrayal.

"I was in Kabul when the brass called me in to say Adrienne had been killed by a roadside bomb during a convoy." His voice broke. "And when I think about how we left things? The last words I spoke to her…"

Darcy got up and sat next to him. "I'm so sorry, Jax." She touched his arm.

"I was flown back to the base in Germany. Mom and Dad came." His mouth wobbled. "I was a mess for a long time."

She nudged him. "Still are."

He exhaled with a shaky laugh. "I have always been able to count on you, Darce, to not allow me to take myself too seriously."

"You know I live to deflate that ego of yours, Jax." But she hugged his arm against her side.

"Mom and Dad took care of Brody until I could wrap up my military career. At Christmas, when they found out about Anna's pregnancy, they flew home. Mom told me it was time to be the dad Brody needed."

Darcy twined her fingers into his. "You are a great father to Brody."

"Not for a while, though." His shoulders rose and fell. "Adrienne's father offered me a job in one of his companies." He swallowed. "A desk job."

Jaxon Pruitt wasn't wired to live his life indoors. "That had to be torture for you."

"I stuck it out because I wanted Brody to know Adrienne's family. But their idea of child rearing was different than mine. And you're right, I was— am—still a mess. With his every need seemingly met by the nanny they hired, I drifted farther and farther from my son." He gulped. "His every need met, except his need for his father."

The grief in Jax's eyes tore at her heart.

"I failed him, Darce, when he needed me the most."

"But you're here now, Jax."

"I didn't realize how much I'd missed this place…" He studied Darcy's hand, his thumb moving back and forth across her skin. "How much I'd missed home and friends like you, Darce."

He'd never touched her like this before. Her resolve crumbled like dunes in a nor'easter. She needed to breathe. This was Jax Pruitt. The gesture didn't mean to him what it meant to her.

Whatever she was feeling was a mistake. Not only for her, but for Brody, too. Jax could take care of himself. He always had. She was just the girl next door, the pastor's kid, his sister's best friend.

Temporary business associates. Nothing more. Because she was leaving. Leaving to start her own new life, her own second chance.

A grieving military widower and his too-cute son were not part of her future. They were friends. Jax had said so himself. Friends she could do. Friends was all she could ever do.

She removed her shoulder from his. "By summer's end, everything will have worked itself out. You'll see."

His dark brown eyes suddenly became unfathomable. It was harder to breathe, much less think, when he looked at her like that.

She gave his hand a quick squeeze and release.

"I'll have worked myself out of a job." Slowly, she eased out of his clasp. "You won't even miss me when I'm gone."

Rising, she stuck her hands in her pockets. So they no longer felt so empty.

He laid the album aside. "You're wrong about one thing."

At the door, she glanced over her shoulder. "What's that?"

"I will miss you."

Stumbling into the hall, she felt her heart skip a beat.

Working with Jax every day. Getting more and more attached to his son. She already cared more about both of them than she should.

Because by summer's end, she had a dreadful feeling it would be her heart that was shattered.

Chapter Ten

Things between him and Darcy subtly altered after his illness. Citing the sunset paddle, she'd called his mom and excused herself not long after he put away the memory album.

Jax recovered and returned to work. Things between him and Brody also changed. Deepened.

He kept Brody by his side as often as he could unless paddling. The little boy became his shadow. And Jax discovered parenting wasn't so much about book knowledge as it was on-the-job training.

Brody held out his hand. "Me do, pweese?"

Gripping the water hose, he glanced at the outfit his son had chosen today. They'd taken to watching baseball games at night together on television. He was teaching Brody the finer points of America's national pastime.

The little man looked ready to take the field in a Little Slugger shirt and shorts. Behind the store,

Brody wriggled his toes in the mud beneath the kayak Jax had hosed off.

Brody's feet would need as much hosing off as the equipment.

"Pweese…"

"Okay." Jax passed him the hose. "But point it toward—ahh!" Brody, hand on the trigger, sprayed Jax's shirt.

"Sowee, Daddy."

He'd never get tired of Brody calling him daddy.

Jax grinned. "What's a little water between guys, huh?" He ruffled Brody's hair. "We won't melt." He beat his chest with his fist. "We're Shoremen."

Brody beat his own small chest. "We Show-men, Daddy."

"Shor-r-rrmen, Brody."

"Show-w-wmen, Daddy."

Jax sighed.

At the sound of a rumbling engine, Brody threw down the hose, which narrowly missed Jax's toes. He hopped back. "Watch it, son."

But Brody took off running toward the parking lot. "Dawcy!"

After stepping over the coiled hose, Jax rounded the corner and froze. The breath in his lungs left him in a whoosh of air.

Brody, as usual, hugged Darcy's knees. And Darcy?

Jax's heart took off at a furious clip. This wasn't the Darcy he was accustomed to seeing.

In open-toed, high heel sandals, she'd gone fancy. In the sea breeze, her strawberry blonde hair fluttered in soft waves around her bare shoulders.

Was that makeup on her face? Yes. He blinked. Yes, it was. Eyeliner, mascara, a hint of blush and a pale pink lip gloss.

Dangly turquoise earrings and a pendant necklace complemented the sundress, the hem flirting with her kneecaps. Nothing like her usual T-shirt, shorts and flip-flops.

As a kid, he'd wondered if tomboy Darcy could do girl. Question answered. He gulped. She could.

Very well, in fact. Darcy had put him on the schedule to lead the Saturday morning paddle, taking a rare day off. And running his hands through his disheveled hair, he became aware of his less-than-put-together appearance.

He probably smelled like marsh mud, and thanks to Brody, he was soaking wet. Speaking of which—

"Uh, Brode. You're going to get Darcy dirty."

Breaking off her animated conversation with his son, she looked at Jax, her arms around Brody. Who was still hugging her knees, effectively preventing her from moving without taking a tumble.

She cupped Brody's upturned cheek. "What's a little dirt between friends, right?"

The gesture, so tender and genuine, seemed

somehow so right to Jax. So right he had to swallow past the boulder lodged in his throat.

Brody released his hold on her knees, but reached for her hand. "Dawcy wook pwetty, Daddy." His son—and Darcy—turned to him.

Okay, his turn to speak. "Yeah."

He stuffed his hand in his pockets. Where was the renowned Pruitt charm when he needed it?

She arched her brow. "Thanks. Hope that compliment didn't cause too much pain."

Red crept up his neck. "Darcy, I—"

Tossing her hair over her shoulder, she moved past him to the porch. Recovering his manners, he yanked open the door for her.

Brody showed him up, though, when he made a sweeping motion with his arm. "Wadies fuwst." A gesture highly reminiscent of Grandpa Everett.

She smiled. "What a little gentleman."

And unlike the sweet look she'd given his son, she sent Jax a look that implied how sadly lacking he was in comparison. Not true at all. He'd always felt Darcy Parks brought out the chivalry in him.

"I thought you said you needed the day off?" He winced, making it sound as if she were unwanted. When actually he'd been thinking of nothing else but her.

Her heels clipping across the linoleum, she hurried to the counter. Brody drifted to the life jacket bin. Mr. Me Do was determined to master the buckles.

"I couldn't find my…" She rummaged through the shelf below the cash register. "Thank goodness." She held up her wallet. "I forgot it after the sunset paddle last night."

And then it hit Jax square in the solar plexus why she was so dressed up.

Darcy had a date.

Somehow he'd imagined she'd always be the same sunshine summer girl he'd always known. But she was different. More than he could have imagined.

He crossed his arms. "So where're you headed?"

A tick of silence passed. She tilted her head. He became mesmerized by the sway of her earrings.

"I'm going across the bridge to Harbor Park in Norfolk. To watch the Tides play."

The gnawing curiosity inside Jax was about to eat him alive. He flexed his jaw. "You're not going to a ball game in that getup."

She looked at him down the length of her deliciously freckled nose. A feat, considering he topped her by eight inches. "We're going to dinner on the pier first."

We're.

Going rigid, he flushed. A deafening noise clamored inside his head. Why, when he'd spilled his guts the other day, had she not thought it important to mention she was part of a "we"? Embarrassment mounted into indignation.

While he'd been fighting for his country—*get-*

ting married and having a kid, too, his conscience chided—Darcy was in a relationship. Probably had been for a while. Why had no one told him? Where was the oft-touted Kiptohanock grapevine when a guy really needed it?

Jax's chest squeezed, making it hard to breathe. "Does the reverend know what you're wearing?"

Her eyes widened and sparked fire. "There's nothing wrong with what I'm wearing."

Jax snorted. "Not enough at the bottom." He waved his hand. "And definitely not enough at the top."

She did that head bobbing thing teenagers did. "Not that it's any of your business," she hissed. "But my father, the Reverend Harold Parks—"

Jax flinched.

"—doesn't have a problem with what I'm wearing." She propped her hand on her shapely hip. "And therefore, neither should you. You're Anna's older brother, Jaxon Pruitt, not mine."

No forgetting that, especially with the peculiar pressure pinching his chest. The bell above the door jangled, and they both swiveled. Ethan Savage's broad shoulders filled the frame.

Surrounded by a sea of orange PFDs, Brody was enjoying himself, clipping and unclipping buckles. Jax bit back a sigh. He knew who'd be picking those up.

Ethan's craggy features creased in a smile. "Hey, Darce."

Jax reeled. Who did Ethan Savage think he was, coming here, calling her that? Which was ridiculous. Like Jax had some sort of monopoly on her name.

Ethan high-fived Brody. "Hey, little Jax Pruitt."

Brody laughed. "Me not Jax. Me Bwody."

As for the smile Darcy beamed Ethan Savage's way? Sucker-punched, Jax felt his jaw drop.

Ethan clapped a friendly hand on Jax's shoulder. "Your family must be thrilled that you're back."

Yeah, he was back, all right. He squared his shoulders, knocking off Ethan's paw.

But Ethan didn't notice. He'd moved on to give Darcy a one-armed hug. "Just wanted to let you know I was outside."

Was it his imagination or did Ethan hold Darcy a little too close? Too close for his liking, Jax could practically feel the muscle ticking in his cheek.

"I had to find my wallet."

Arm still around her, Ethan nodded his blond head. "No rush, Darce. We've got plenty of time." Still hugging…

Jax ground his teeth. Just about the time he'd decided to remove that arm from Darcy's shoulder himself, Ethan stepped away.

"I'll be in the car." The ex-army ranger headed toward the door. "Whenever you two are finished."

"We're finished."

Oh no, they weren't. His hand shot out and took

hold of Darcy's arm. Only just stopping her from following Ethan Savage out the door.

She glanced from his hand to his face. "What?"

Jax scrunched his nose. "Didn't realize you and Ryan's little brother were so chummy."

"He was two grades behind Anna and me in school." Darcy glared at Jax. "What's your problem today?"

He scowled right back.

"I'm leaving my SUV for my dad. He's over at the church as usual. But he promised to take a look at the engine. It's acting up."

A vein pulsed in Jax's throat, matching the beat in his cheek. "I'll take a look at your engine. Your dad has many fine qualities, but fixing motors isn't one of them."

"Suit yourself." She not so gently removed her hand from his grasp. "Justine's probably getting hot out there in the car."

"Justine?" He frowned. "Ethan's sister?"

"Ethan. Justine." She unfurled her fingers, ticking off the names. "Luke. And me. We're going to the baseball game."

Brody's head popped up. "Me wike basebaw, Dawcy."

So did Jax. Something must've shown on his face.

Darcy bit her lip. "We've had the tickets for nearly two months. I didn't know you'd be here when we bought them."

He leaned against the counter with a dizzying

sense of relief. A relief he didn't care to examine too closely. This wasn't a date.

Unless Ethan bringing along his older sister and younger brother counted. Admittedly, it'd been a long time for Jax. But back in his day, that hadn't constituted a date.

With an irritated look, she nudged him off balance. Kind of like how he'd felt since the first day they started working together.

"Are you absolutely incapable of standing upright?" She blew by him, swooping over to Brody.

To his son's delight, she tickled his tummy and rained kisses on his skinny little neck. Jax tried not to envy him. And failed.

Getting to her feet, she adjusted her purse strap. "Someday, Brody, we'll go to a game, I promise."

But she was looking at Jax. Someday... His heart ratcheted up a notch.

"Until then, Darcy..." Eyebrow arched, he deliberately leaned against the counter once more and gave her his trademark Jaxon Pruitt half-mast stare. "...try not to stay out too late. PKs have church tomorrow."

Teeth grinding, she did an about-face. The dress whirled around her toned legs. And sauntering to the door, somehow she managed to capture the swagger Jax had believed all his. And in heels.

His stomach did a nosedive. Little Darcy Parks, all grown up. And then she was gone, bell jingling, slamming the door behind her.

Click, snap, click went the buckles on the life vest. "Dawcy pwetty, Daddy."

Out of the mouths of babes. Jax let out a breath, deflated. "Yes, she is, Brode."

Why hadn't he told her how wonderful she looked? Like a ray of sunshine on a cloudy day. Wasn't there a song that went like that?

Oh, yeah. "My Girl." But by no stretch of the imagination was Darcy his girl. His mouth went dry. Did he want her to be?

He'd learned his lesson, or so he believed, with Adrienne. Good thing he'd sworn off women and relationships. Though Darcy was nothing like Adrienne. A realization that was both frightening and thrilling.

Darcy was a whole different story. She'd always had an uncanny ability to penetrate the game face bravado he presented to the rest of the world. There was no defense against her. Or the way she made him feel.

Extracting himself from the floatation devices, Brody ambled over. "What wong, Daddy?"

"Nothing, son." Jax exhaled again. "Daddy's just being a bigger idiot than usual."

Good thing she was leaving in September.

But suddenly summer's end seemed far too close.

Chapter Eleven

At the shop a few weeks later, Darcy restocked the first aid kit. Every day, Jax took more ownership of the business as she handed off additional responsibilities to him. The upcoming corporate weekend retreat would be his first overnight paddle. And he'd serve as expedition leader.

He was a quick study. Either that, or eager to get rid of her. As eager to get rid of her as she was to get rid of him? On her part, not true. Grownup Jax had proved to be even more dangerous to her sensibilities.

With the sunshine glinting off the water like diamonds, she relished having the shop to herself in the mornings. But for only a few months longer. Her stomach knotted.

She'd arranged their schedules so Jax had time to take Brody to the Pruitts' house before arriving at the shop midday. Sticking to her resolve to avoid Jax whenever possible, she made sure her shift ended as soon as he arrived.

Afternoons, he oversaw Ozzie and Savannah's tours. When the shop closed at five, he left to pick up Brody. And Chas came on board to conduct the ever-popular summer sunset or full-moon paddles. The latter were Jax's idea, proving popular not only with the tourists, but locals, too.

She glanced out to the dock. On a clamming expedition, a family of six paddled behind Savannah. The line of kayaks soon emerged on the other side of the busy marina traffic, Ozzie in the rear.

Darcy drifted to the front window. Cars and trucks filled the Sandpiper parking lot. The usual crowd included her father, an honorary member of the ROMEOs—retired older men eating out.

She relished the simple rhythm of small town life. Was she crazy to long for somewhere else? Or was the longing not so much for another place as a longing for something—someone—else?

Darcy jolted when the bell above the door jingled. As Jax sauntered inside, the tranquility of the morning was broken.

She grimaced. "You're early."

He threw her an insolent grin. "Miss me?"

"Pitter patter goes my heart."

His lips twitched. "I live to please."

She sighed. With his cheeky grin, laughing eyes and wind-ruffled hair, Jax was all too pleasing to the eyes. Way too appealing for her peace of mind. This would not do. This would not do at all.

A niggle of panic wormed its way into her thoughts. Maybe she could turn the business over to him earlier than Labor Day. Keep her distance till then. She and Jax functioned best at arm's length. Always had, always would.

She went over the details of the overnighter with him while they waited for the executives across the bay to arrive. A maroon van pulled into the parking lot.

"You're on, Jax." She gathered supplies in her arms. "Time for you to work that Pruitt charm."

He cocked his head. "Does it work on you?"

She sniffed, heading outside.

The corporate execs, male and female, ranged in age from early thirties to late fifties. She and Jax spent the first few minutes gauging their experience in the water. They assigned kayaks, lined up on the shoreline like brightly colored crayons in a box.

Jax showed the group how to rotate their strokes, using the large muscles of their torsos to propel the blades through the water.

Standing next to Darcy, a petite brunette awkwardly rotated the blade of her smaller shafted paddle. "I spend my life trying to keep pace with these guys. Will I be able to do this?"

"One of the great things about kayaking is you don't need much upper-arm strength to become an excellent paddler." Darcy adjusted the strap on the woman's PFD. "It's all about technique, which we'll teach you over the next few days."

Packing the kayaks was an art form. Food, camping gear and the zip-top plastic bags to carry out the all-important toilet paper after necessity stops. Kiptohanock Kayaking prided itself on being a green company, leaving no trace behind on its seaside ecotours.

She explained to the group how to stow the dry bag with their most important possessions in the compartment behind the hatch. Including snack food for energy and water bottles to prevent dehydration. With coverage spotty along the coast, there was no need for cell phones.

"Everyone at some point is going to get wet," Jax cautioned. "Therefore, we plan for it and learn how to recover from it."

Her cue. She adjusted the floatable Croakie straps on her sunglasses behind her ears. She pushed the extra kayak they used to demonstrate a wet exit into the water and got in.

At her nod, he turned to the execs. "Hanging upside down in the water may seem terrifying at first…"

One of the men gave a nervous laugh. "At first?"

"Your goal is to remain calm and not panic." Jax waded waist-deep into the water. "We're going to demonstrate the best way to flip."

The department supervisor crossed his arms. "Like there's ever a good way to flip?"

More sheepish laughter sounded.

Darcy pressed the outside of her legs against the interior panels of the kayak. "Not panicking is key. Flipped kayaks can be righted with a little know-how."

Jax placed his hands on the bow of her boat. "So when you sense the kayak becoming unbalanced, lean forward…"

Darcy slanted forward, until her forehead almost touched the deck.

"Maintain this tucked position while underwater. Hold your breath. Exhale through your nose."

She pounded her hands on the hull of the craft. "It's important to make some noise to alert your fellow kayakers about what's happened."

"Now we're going to show you from beginning to end what to do." His gaze darted to hers. "Ready?"

A not-so-tiny step toward trusting him. Her heart thudded. "Ready."

When he flipped the boat, she went sideways and the murky water rushed to meet her. Though not unexpected, she still flinched at the coolness against her skin. And then she was upside down. Holding on to the kayak and using her hips, she completed the roll in a smooth motion. Her head cleared the water first.

Rivulets of water streamed down her face. Applause erupted. Although it had felt like she'd been underwater for a decade, the maneuver properly executed had her submerged less than five seconds. She blew a tendril of hair out of her eyes.

Jax's brow creased. "Are you okay?"

"I'm good."

He pulled her ashore. "That's not a news flash to me, Darce." As he helped her out of the kayak his breath stirred her hair.

A sea breeze wafted, bringing the scents of sandalwood, sunscreen and him to her nostrils. Her cheeks heated. Arm's length didn't seem to be working. She retrieved her Squamish.

Once everyone got into the water, Jax kept the group in close formation. They made good time paddling north on the water trail. Pleased exclamations broke out as the kayaks rounded the lighthouse point.

Jax glided closer to Darcy. "You say a family lives there now?"

She rested her paddle across the cockpit, allowing the paddlers time for photos. "Caroline Duer's husband, Weston Clark, renovated the lighthouse and keeper's cottage a few years ago."

Jax's smile faltered. "I've missed more than I realized."

"You and Brody will be back in the swing of things before you know it." In the turquoise waters of the Keys, she'd be the one missing Kiptohanock. Not so happy a realization for Darcy.

Halfway between Kiptohanock and the famous Chincoteague ponies, he led the kayaks toward the uninhabited barrier island they used for overnighting.

Aiming for the beach, Darcy paddled hard until her kayak made contact with the sand. After jumping out, she helped the others beach their boats. In disembarking, more than one client got wet, though.

"No worries." Jax dragged the kayaks higher, out of reach of the incoming tide. "Hardest thing about kayaking is getting in and getting out."

He got everyone started on pitching the pup tents. Unpacking a dry sack she pulled from a storage compartment, Darcy held up a bag of marshmallows and a slew of chocolate bars. "S'mores after dinner."

"Who doesn't love chocolate?" He loaded his arms with pots and pans. "I should build a bonfire by the creek one night, Darce. I don't think Brody's ever had a s'more."

She gathered the rest of the supplies. "He'd love that."

"That's not all he loves." Jax chuckled. "You've made a place for yourself in his heart. Of course, he's not the only one who appreciates Kiptohanock's favorite PK."

She trudged up the incline without comment.

He unloaded near the blackened fire pit. "I'll carry the Coleman next."

She bristled. "I'm perfectly capable—"

"Don't get your red hairs in a tizzy. I got it."

She folded her arms. "I am *not* a redhead."

His mouth quirked. "Sure you are."

"I'm not." And to prove it, she held a lock of hair to the sun. "Strawberry blonde. Emphasis on blonde."

"Blonde…" He rolled his tongue in his cheek. "Whatever you say, Darce. I love it when you go all—" he made quote marks in the air with his fingers "—*strawberry blonde* on me."

She pursed her lips.

"Your turn." He winked. "Tell me what you love about me, Darce."

She shifted, her feet sinking in the sandy soil. He was in one of his goading moods. Time to take Jax Pruitt's ego down a peg or two.

"Like the I'm-God's-gift-to-women attitude?" She curled her lip. "I think not." She turned toward the brush. "We need sticks for the s'mores."

"I'll help."

"You remind me of a sandbur, Jax." She handed him a stick. "Tenaciously annoying. A real pain in the—"

He raised an eyebrow. "Such language from a PK."

"—heel." She smirked.

Jax's lips curved. "So you're saying I'm your Achilles' heel."

"You're more like these sand fleas." She swatted the air between them. "Irritating and..." She frowned.

"It's okay to admit you like me, Darce."

She recoiled. "Like you?"

He grinned, gathering more sticks. "You like a lot of things about me."

"That's not true."

"Sure it is. You like my kid—"

"Probably the only thing likable about you, Jaxon, is your kid."

"You liked my lime-green freezer pops."

Her mouth rounded. "You gave up the lime-green freezer pop for me?"

Jax smiled, towering over her. "You like my mom and dad. You like my brothers and sister. You like my house." He tilted his head. "You liked when I made a touchdown."

She sucked in a breath, her eyes wide. He'd known that?

"You liked everything about me. Hence, you liked *me*. You liked when we played pirate and clashed swords—"

"Still do. I mean..." She gulped. "We still clash swords."

He straightened, satisfaction written across his face. "Because you *like* me, Darcy."

"I do not." She jutted her chin. "You, Jaxon

Pruitt, are a necessary evil to getting off the Shore for good."

She'd like to wipe the smirk right off his face. She didn't like Jaxon. Maybe once, she'd cared for the boy he'd been. But now?

Like seemed too small an emotion for the way he made her feel. But if not like, then what was left? She certainly didn't love him. Did she?

Gasping, she turned and fell face-first across a log laying on the path.

"Darcy!"

Of all the humiliating—

"Darcy, are you okay?"

"I'm fine," she growled, spitting sand. Pushing her palms against the ground, she rolled onto her side.

The others peered over Jax's shoulder. She scowled. She'd made a spectacle of herself. "Give me room."

He reached for her. "Darce…"

Using her knee, she pushed to her feet. A sharp pain shot through her ankle. Her leg buckled, but he caught her arm in his strong grip.

"You're not fine," he grunted.

Darcy flushed twelve shades of red.

"Stop being stubborn and let me help you." Cupping her elbow, he pressed her against his side. "You're hurt. Don't make things worse."

Tears stung her eyelids. Why did everything always go wrong when she was with Jax?

His tone softened. "Darcy…please…"

There wasn't a woman alive who could resist Jax when he used that cajoling, sweet tone. Herself included. Who was she kidding? Herself most of all.

Why her most of all? Probably because Jax was so seldom sweet. Seldom allowing anyone to see the genuine kindness behind the always charming, devil-may-care attitude he donned like Kevlar.

It was a sweetness his son possessed in spades. A sweetness she'd not glimpsed since that long-ago summer when—

She took a shuddery breath. "Don't need an audience, Jax."

"You heard the boss, ladies and gentlemen. She's fine. Get those tents up."

The execs drifted away.

Her eyebrow rose. "Boss, huh?"

"I am your humble servant."

"Since when?"

He wound his fingers into the hair at the nape of her neck. She placed her palm on his chest to shove him away. But when she felt the pounding of his heart, she didn't push.

"Since…" He leaned closer. A muscle throbbed in his cheek. His gaze lingered on her lips. But he removed his hand, plucking a stray leaf out of her hair.

"I'm a mess." She probably smelled of bug

spray and sweat. No wonder she didn't have a boyfriend.

His eyes crinkled, the skin fanning at the corners. "I like messes."

The Pruitt charm, she told herself, fighting not to blush.

"I want to take a look at your ankle to make sure you're really okay and not just being your usual obstinate self."

"So touched by your concern, Jax." But with a firm grip on his arm, she hopped on her good leg and allowed him to lead her toward the clearing around the fire pit.

He fell to his knees beside her. "Let me see." He bent over her foot.

She inhaled sharply as he eased off her Croc.

His head snapped up. "I didn't mean to hurt—"

"Sorry to be such a drama queen."

His forehead puckered. "You're the toughest girl I know. But you don't have to hide your feelings." He rested his hands on his knees. "Not with me."

If only that were true.

"Try to rotate your ankle."

Wincing, she complied.

"I don't think it's broken." His fingers, warm on her skin, stroked her foot. "I think you may've sprained it. We're going to have to RICE it."

She gritted her teeth. "I know the drill. Rest, ice, compress and elevate."

He sat on his heels. "Not so fun when the shoe is on the other foot, huh?"

"You took my shoe." She glared. "I hate being one of those helpless females."

Jax laughed. "You've never been helpless in your life, Darcy Parks. As for female?"

His quick, stomach-quivering grin robbed her of breath. "I've always been glad you weren't one of the boys, Darce."

She also wasn't accustomed to having other people waiting on her.

"Get used to it," he growled, and insisted she remain stationary against the driftwood log he propped behind her back.

Then he made dinner. Her shoulders sagged. What good was she? Jax and Kiptohanock Kayaking didn't need her anymore.

After dinner, he drifted down beside her on the sand. Everyone gathered around the bonfire to roast marshmallows and make s'mores. Resulting in lots of laughter, melted chocolate and gooey fingers.

"If you don't mind…" She darted her eyes at Jax. "Since my mouth still works…"

"Ain't that the truth." He mashed a toasted marshmallow between two graham crackers.

She ignored him. "I'd like to share with y'all a few Eastern Shore legends."

He smiled as she told stories ranging from pirates—they both liked pirates—to tales they'd heard from their grandparents about German U boats. Eventually, the weary corporate kayakers trooped off to their tents. An easy, companionable silence fell.

She ought to get some sleep, but made no real attempt to leave the beach. Water lapped against the shore. Frogs croaked in the maritime forest. From somewhere in the dark, the scent of honeysuckle floated. Very nice. Very summer.

Who was she kidding? Jax's long legs stretched out beside her made the beach more than nice tonight. His shoulder brushed against hers, and Darcy's heart raced. *Get a grip.*

This was Jax.

Exactly. This was *Jax*.

She needed to move away. What had happened to keeping her distance? Good thing she'd be gone in a few months. She slumped against the log.

Jax broke the silence first. "The only downside to guiding these multiday excursions?" He impaled the stick into the sand. "I miss Brody."

Forgetting her no-touching policy, she rubbed his arm. "Give him a few years and Brody will be able to go with you."

"Next time maybe Dad could drive Brody here." Jax stared at her hand. "And he could spend the night in the tent with me."

Jax made no attempt to move. The firelight flickered across his face, outlining the rugged bone structure. His handsome mouth…

Darcy fought the urge to finger the cleft in his chin. How many lonely nights had she spent wishing, dreaming, for someone like Jax to share the bonfire with? Truth be told, not just someone... Her breath hitched. Unconsciously, had she been wishing for Jax?

"Whatever happened to the adventurous girl pirate who was going to kayak the Amazon? Surf the North Shore? Hike the Inca Trail?"

"You remember that?" She blew out a breath. "Pretty silly, huh?"

"Not silly. It's who you are, Darce." He stared into the flickering flames. "I like who you are."

She swallowed. "Thank you, Jax. I like... I—I appreciate you sharing your freezer pops with me."

"Don't strain yourself, Darce."

She took a deep breath. "And I appreciate you sharing your mom and your dad. Your house. Your sister and brothers."

"I appreciate you sharing the tree house with us." He cleared his throat. "With me."

"You're welcome."

He poked a stick into the embers of the fire, sending sparks shooting skyward. "I like your dreams, Darcy. I've always thought it would be kind of cool to hike to Machu Picchu. Or scuba dive a pirate shipwreck in the Caribbean."

"I'm not as brave as you, Jax. Half of me wants to see what else is out there." She rested her chin on her up-drawn knees. "And the other half can't bear to leave what I love that's here."

"Staying might be the bravest thing of all." He pressed his shoulder against hers. "Where I went wrong from the start. And neither Adrienne or I were brave enough to fight for each other." His voice deepened. "But that's a mistake I won't make again, I promise you."

Was he thinking of that last summer morning all those years ago? No, he couldn't mean that. He was talking about his son. Of course he meant his son. He'd never walk away from Brody.

She blinked moisture from her eyes. PKs didn't cry. At least not in public. She must be more tired or hurt—her ankle, that is—than she'd realized.

"I think it's time to call it a night."

Scrambling to his feet, he took her arm. "Let me help…"

"At your peril, Pruitt."

His smile was a sword lashing her heart. "I'm willing to take the risk."

But as he helped her over to her tent and said good-night, she acknowledged that the real heart in peril was her own.

The next morning she one-footed it out of the tent, to find Jax waiting for her on the other side of the flap. Eyes crinkling, he offered his arm, Prince Charming that he was.

"Morning," she grunted, but took his elbow. Violating the no-touch rule yet again.

The paddlers downed the breakfast he'd made, and he'd already repacked the kayaks.

She sighed. "You don't need me anymore, Jax."

"I *do* need you." He frowned. "I mean, Brody needs you. He's come so far."

Brody...

She lifted her chin. "Everyone about ready to head out?" She eyed the distance to her beached kayak. This was going to be tricky. "Jax, if I could use your arm for support I think I can hobble—"

Darcy gasped as he swept her into his arms. "What are you doing?" Pressed against his shirt, could he feel the thundering of her heart?

He took a step.

"Jax..." Balance shifting, she wrapped her arms around his neck.

"Much better." He strode past the fire pit.

"Jax... Put me down." Level with his jawline, she experienced a sudden longing to rest her cheek against his beard stubble.

He plowed across the sand. "I like you here."

She liked being here—in his arms.

"Getting in and out is the hardest, remember?" He tucked her into the kayak. "Do you need a tow?"

With reluctance, she loosened her arms from around his neck. "It's my ankle, not my biceps. I can make it on my own."

A faint smile touched his lips. "Like Brody. Got it." Short tendrils of damp dark hair curled at the base of his neck.

Her lungs emptied.

Jax handed over the paddle. "Does this mean you've forgiven me?"

As if not forgiving him had ever really been an option. The new, improved, mature Jax that she liked so much.

Throwing caution—and good sense?—to the wind, she made a new resolution. To let go of past summers. And to enjoy the rest of whatever summer they had ahead of them. She nodded.

With a bemused expression on his face, he gently pushed her kayak into the water. "Thank you, Darcy."

They drifted apart, still gazing at each other until somebody called Jax's name, and he jerked. His muscles strained under his T-shirt as he carried another kayak to the water.

And suddenly, Darcy had the uncomfortable feeling life in the Keys might not be the only dream God had placed in her heart.

Chapter Twelve

It was a perfect day for the annual Fourth of July celebration. White puffy clouds dotted the blue sky. Jax and Brody had gotten a later-than-intended start—the reality of single parenthood.

He hadn't seen Darcy in a few days. For once, she'd taken his advice: to stay off her ankle and let it heal. But he'd missed her. A lot. Too much?

Cars lined Seaside Road. Parking was going to be a problem. He did a slow drive-by of the kayaking shop to be sure everything was okay.

He spotted a colorful array of kayaks paddling across the harbor. Chas and the others had everything under control.

Barring any emergencies, today was about Jax spending his all-time favorite holiday with his son. Their first Fourth of July together.

With the road around the green closed to traffic, he took a side street and parked in front of his parents' empty house.

His folks were already at the festivities. Evy was running the Firecracker Book Sale, and Charlie was on duty somewhere.

Once unbuckled, Brody scrambled out. "Dawcy?" Her house appeared as unoccupied as the Pruitts' place.

"She's not there, buddy."

Brody's lip poked out. "Me miss her."

Him, too. "How about we get something to eat?"

Brody's frown turned upside down. "Me hungwy."

Jax bit back a smile. Worked every time. He wasn't sure what he would've done with a daughter. In some ways, boys were easier.

Puffing out his chest, Brody refused to allow his father to carry him to the square. "Me big, Daddy." But he tucked his hand into Jax's. And smiled.

Jax's heart melted.

Hand in hand—thanks to Darcy—father and son strolled toward the center of town. They emerged on the north side of the green to find the square had been transformed. Inside the gazebo, bedecked in patriotic bunting, a community band played strains of "This Is My Country."

Mounted on corner lampposts, red, white and blue ribbons fluttered in the breeze. Small American flags lined the sidewalks. Artisans had set up their colorful wares on tables scattered throughout the green.

Children dashed everywhere. The aromas of fried dough, barbecue and clam burgers wafted across the green. Brody's stomach growled. Wending their way around lawn chairs, they got in line at a food truck to order.

They didn't have to wait long. Sack in hand, Jax scanned the crowd, failing to spot the one face…

He was as pathetic as his son, searching for the strawberry blonde who'd managed to make a home in his son's heart. His, too? Jax scowled.

"Anybody ever tell you one day your face is going to freeze like that?"

Darcy scooped Brody into her arms, and smiled at him.Jax's heart lurched when she smiled at him, too.

"And then you'll lose your touch with the women for good."

"Long time no see, Darce."

She tickled Brody's belly. "Whatcha eating, Brode?"

His son arched his back, squealing with laughter.

Remembering the touch of her hand at the beach the other day, Jax felt his cheeks warm. He cleared his throat. "French fries and burgers."

Brody rested his chin on her shoulder.

She tilted her head, tucking his head against her neck. And Jax missed a breath at the sweetness of her totally unconscious gesture. They were so achingly perfect together.

"Where are y'all sitting, Jax?"

Only with difficulty did he bring himself back from the idyllic image his son in Darcy's arms painted.

"Um…" He peered around the crowded green. "I should've brought chairs."

Brody nuzzled Darcy's neck with his cheek. She kissed the top of his son's head, and Jax thought his heart might explode.

"M-maybe we'll eat at the house," he stammered.

"And miss the fun?" Her eyes sparkled, teasing him. "Why don't you and Brody come eat with us?"

"I couldn't—"

"Yay, Dawcy." Brody bounced in her arms.

"It's settled then."

"Darcy, I—"

"Unless you've made plans to meet someone." The light in her eyes faded.

"No plans." He touched her arm. A mistake. Something as strong as an electrical current shot through his fingertips, jolting them both. His pulse raced.

She stared at his hand on her arm. "No plans for Jax Pruitt might be a first," she whispered.

"There's no one else."

No one but you, he wanted to shout. But he

didn't. After what happened with Adrienne, he couldn't.

"You'd be doing me a favor." Her eyes fastened on his mouth before she tore her gaze away. "You know my mom. There's only so many deviled eggs and so much fried chicken a girl can eat without losing her figure."

"There's nothing wrong with your figure."

He blinked, surprised at himself. She blinked back, as surprised as he.

"Me wike eggs, Daddy."

She settled big boy Brody on her hip. Not too big to be toted by Darcy. "Follow me then."

Darcy led them past Fourth of July revelers to a floral quilt on the church end of the square. She deposited Brody beside the wicker basket. Lithe as always, she folded her legs under her and sat down. She pulled out a plate of deviled eggs.

"Where are your folks?" Jax was desperately fighting not to get too attached to the cozy vision of Darcy playing with his son in the grass.

"Dad's making the rounds as usual. Mom and the Independence Day committee are probably putting the finishing touches on the parade."

He dropped to his knees. "My parents, too."

Darcy held out a plate of chicken. As he reached for it, she pulled back. "Unless you'd rather eat the burgers."

He lunged, grabbing the plate. "Are you kidding

me? Lose a chance at Agnes Parks's cooking? Do you know me at all?"

"Not as well as I thought." She handed Brody a hush puppy. "Not as much as I'd like." And she blushed, dropping her eyes.

His heart clanged painfully against his ribs. To distract himself, he popped a deviled egg into his mouth and chewed. A stream of Kiptohanock residents stopped to say hello. Darcy was like everybody's kid sister, dear niece and surrogate daughter.

But to him, so much more.

Jax sipped sweet tea from a red plastic cup. Darcy and her parents were well-liked. It wasn't hard to see why. Barefoot, legs crossed, she laughed at something Izzie Clark said in passing.

The only thing marring the perfection of the day was how Darcy kept describing to everyone the beachfront apartment she was moving into come September. His gut churned as he listened to details of her soon-to-be blissful new life in Florida.

He put down the chicken leg, his appetite suddenly gone. "Where's Margaret Davenport?" He craned his neck. "Doesn't the queen of the Kiptohanock grapevine usually run these community gatherings? Or have things really changed since I left?"

Darcy repacked the leftovers. "As a PK, there's

a lot I can't discuss, as you know. But at this point, it's general knowledge."

"Nothing's happened to her, I hope. She's bossy and a meddler, but she's our bossy meddler."

"Margaret's fine." Darcy ran her finger around the rim of her cup. "Physically, at least. But on New Year's, her absentee husband ran off with his secretary."

Jax's mouth fell open. "I'd forgotten she even had a husband."

"Even though they'd been unhappily married for decades and living separate lives, naturally she was devastated by the divorce."

He looked away. "No one wants to be a failure."

Darcy's eyes flicked to his. "Margaret handed off her Fourth of July responsibilities to Mom and the committee. Supposedly she's on a cruise in the Caribbean, reevaluating her life."

Lot of that was going around these days. He could definitely relate, and silently, he wished the indefatigable Margaret well.

The large metal bell on the end of the wharf clanged, and Darcy hopped to her feet. Everyone around them rose.

Jax hoisted Brody into his arms as all eyes turned toward the flagpole at the Coast Guard station. The band fell silent. The American flag crackled, stretching taut in the stiff breeze blowing off the harbor.

Brody hung on to Jax's neck. "Is it time, Daddy?"

His lips quirked, anticipating Darcy's surprise. "Just like we practiced."

"What've you boys been up to now?"

Coast Guard station commander Braeden Scott spoke into the microphone. "Ladies and gentlemen, let us join together in reciting the Pledge of Allegiance."

Brody placed his hand over his heart like they'd practiced. "Me say pwedge, Dawcy."

Everyone stood taller, straighter. As a veteran, Jax raised his hand to his forehead in a salute.

"I pledge allegiance to the flag of the United States of America…" Voices rang out across the green.

Brody lifted his chin. "And to the pubwic for which it stands…"

Her lips curved. "One nation under God. Indivisible."

Brody broadened his skinny shoulders. "With wiberty…"

Her gaze never strayed from the flag, but merriment winked in her eyes.

"And justice for aw." His little chest puffed with pride in a job well done.

She patted Brody's leg. Jax exchanged amused glances with Darcy.

The reverend moved to the mic. "Let us pray."

He gave thanks for their great nation, for the sacrifice of all who safeguarded their country, and for the freedom they enjoyed.

Next, Jax's brother-in-law, Ryan, walked a young Latina girl to the platform. "Maria Guzman will now sing the National Anthem." He adjusted the mic to her height.

She was one of Anna's at-risk students, Jax recalled. Her proud parents and two younger siblings beamed from the sidelines. She had a sweet, clear tone. A hush fell over the audience. Even Brody stilled.

Jax had loved serving his country. Standing there, he remembered friends who'd died in faraway places so he could be here on this perfect July day with his son. And he also thought of Adrienne's sacrifice.

For the first time, thoughts of Adrienne no longer brought a stabbing pain, but gratitude. She'd given him Brody. And despite the turmoil they'd brought each other, he would never regret having his son. He had so much to be grateful for.

A tendril of Darcy's strawberry blonde hair brushed his cheek. Was it possible? Was there still so much to look forward to?

Jax maintained the salute until the last note echoed over the blue-green water.

The church bell rang from the steeple. Darcy watched the play of emotion on Jax's face. The band launched into "America the Beautiful."

She'd never really understood before. He'd been willing to offer his life for the country he loved.

And his wife had made the ultimate sacrifice. What must it be like to be a part of something so much larger than one's self?

Did she love anyone or anything that much? Yes, she loved Jax and Brody enough to sacrifice her life. Stunned at the realization, she blinked rapidly. Was it true?

Somewhere, somehow, this deep, deep liking had become something far more. And it scared Darcy. Terrified her. Because in giving them her love, she gave them the power to also crush her heart.

In the middle of this earth-shattering revelation, Jax's father found them. "I need to borrow the little man for a while." He gave her a one-armed hug. "Hey, Darcy Parks."

To many, the retired deputy sheriff was an intimidating man. But to her, he was a man who'd cheered as loudly for her as he'd cheered for Anna, his daughter. Too often Darcy's own father had been too busy to attend their volleyball games.

Brody held out his arms to his granddad.

Jax cocked his head. "What's going on?"

Everett winked at his grandson. "Never you mind, Jaxon. Brody and I have a surprise planned. We'll see you at the parade."

Just like that, Darcy was left alone with Jax and her new, disturbing feelings for him.

He plopped down on the quilt. "Did you say your mom sent pie?"

Jax grinned. Her stomach took a nosedive. She handed him a slice.

"Doesn't get more American than your mom's apple pie." Taking a bite, he sighed, rolling the flavor in his mouth.

She plucked a blade of grass, twirling it between her fingers. She felt strangely awkward, her feelings raw and exposed.

Her mom bustled over, laying two small flags on the quilt. "For the parade. It's starting soon."

"Miss Agnes, you've outdone yourself." Jax laid his hand over his heart. "There were many Fourths I'd had given a month's wages to have your pie."

What a kiss-up.

But her mom's face lit up, and Darcy smiled, watching him effortlessly work her mother. Then she grimaced. Working her mother like he worked all the ladies.

Agnes patted his cheek as if he were Brody, instead of the hunky, thirty-two-year-old... Darcy fanned herself. She stopped when she saw her mother laughing.

"Don't forget to get a good spot for the parade." Her mom's eyes twinkled. "I have it on good authority there's an entry you don't want to miss." She drifted away to distribute more flags.

Jax dug into the pie. "Do you have any idea about what she and my dad are being so mysterious about?"

Darcy shook her head. "I know a prime location, though, to find out."

After gobbling the last forkful, he sprang to his feet and started gathering the remains of their picnic. He deposited the trash as she led him toward a vantage point on a less crowded side of the square.

With a shout and blare of trumpets, the parade began. The high school marching band—in casual summer attire—performed a swinging "It's a Grand Old Flag." Followed by pets and their owners on leashes. The pets, that is.

Or maybe not. Darcy laughed as a small, but fierce Chihuahua pulled his owner down the block.

Antique cars crawled by. The local beauty queen waved from a flashy convertible. The children's division of wheeled entries came next.

Darcy pointed out the children belonging to people Jax might have a connection to. Like Zander, another one of Anna's at-risk students, whose uncle fixed boats at the marina. And the little guy whose mother worked at the Savage Garden Center—Oscar, peddling madly to keep up with the older children.

Finally, the smallest participants.

She nudged Jax, but he'd already seen the blur of streamers and pinwheels fastened on the Big Wheels. Brody was at the helm, his grandfather trotting alongside. And right behind them, Brody's grandmother pushed Ruby in her stroller.

Brody's little legs pumped, churning the pedals. The grin on his face was huge. "Daddy! Dawcy!" He let go of the handlebars. "Wook at me! Me big!"

The trike wobbled. Everett said something. Brody clamped both hands on the handlebars and the Big Wheels righted itself.

"Not too big too fast, please," Jax whispered.

She looked at him. Saw the pride on his face. The wonder. The love for his son.

"Way to go, Brody." Jax held up the flag, waving it wildly. "I'm so proud of you, son."

Darcy slipped her free hand into his. "I'm so proud of you with Brody."

He squeezed, twining his fingers through hers.

"Wed, white and bwue," Brody called.

"Come on." She tugged at Jax. "Let's follow Brody around the square."

Stepping into the street, they cheered Brody past the fire station, florist shop and church until he reached the finish line.

Later, there was ice cream. As the afternoon wore on, many families went home with cranky, overtired children. Brody lay spread-eagled between Darcy and Jax on the quilt, out for the count. Exhausted from the parade.

Anna and Ryan said their goodbyes as baby Ruby kicked up a fuss.

Jax made a face. "Just like her mother."

Anna stuck out her tongue at him before walking away. "I heard that."

"'Cause I meant you to…"

Darcy rolled her eyes. "Brothers and sisters."

He leaned on his elbows. "We tried our best to make you an honorary Pruitt sibling."

"Is that what I am, Jax? An honorary sister?"

"When we were little, yes." He lay down next to his sleeping son. "Now…not so much." He closed his eyes.

She pulled her knees to her chin and watched him sleep. Uninterrupted, she took her time. Enjoying just looking at him. Appreciating his strong features. The irresistible cleft in his chin.

The lines carved into Jax's face only a month ago had eased. This place was good for him. Good for him and Brody. Home, where they belonged.

Did she belong here anymore? She shut her eyes, and the activity in the square became a distant clamor. In a few months, she'd leave her family, church, Jax and Brody to make a new life for herself.

With the way she felt about Jax, should she leave? Yet because of the way she felt about Jax, could she stay?

Opening her eyes, she found his gaze scanning her face. Her limbs twitched.

"Sorry." She let go of her cramped knees. "I must've fallen asleep." Brody no longer nestled between them. "Where's your little guy?"

Jax stretched out on his side. "Mom and Dad took him to their house. I'll pick him up after the fireworks. He wouldn't like the noise."

"Oh." She ran her fingers through her wind-tangled locks. "You didn't have to stay."

He caught her hand. "I'm right where I want to be."

And so was she. As darkness fell, a local group performed contemporary love songs. Jax got up at one point and returned with two sparklers.

"I figured you'd want one."

She sat up and reached for it. "You know me so well."

Jax lit the sparkler, which flared to life. "Not as well as I'd like."

Her heart did a slow-burning spiral in her chest. He lit the other sparkler for himself. A boom shattered the air, saving her from having to reply.

A blue starburst exploded against the night sky, swirling into a kaleidoscope of color. There were oohs and ahhs.

Their sparklers fizzled out, but other fireworks crackled in quick succession—white, green, pink. Plumes of dazzling light shot skyward over the harbor before falling once more to earth. Then in a tumultuous finale of a dozen rockets, it was over for another year. The acrid scent of gunpowder hung in the thick summer air.

Jax grabbed the handle of the wicker basket and Darcy folded the quilt. It had been the most wonderful Fourth of July she'd ever experienced. And she didn't want it to end.

He escorted her through the departing crowd, her elbow cupped in his hand. She quivered at the touch of his fingers on her skin.

"Cold?"

She wasn't about to admit what his touch did to her equilibrium. To her good sense. They crossed to the residential section.

She sighed. "I should've brought a jacket. The wind off the water can get—"

He stopped on the sidewalk in front of her house. After putting down the basket, he took hold of her bare upper arms.

"Jax...what're you doing?"

The silvery glow of moonlight reflected on his face. On his mouth. On his hooded eyes. "What I should've done a long time ago."

Darcy's legs felt as stable as a jellyfish on land.

His thumb moved across her arm. "I should've told you how much you mean to me, Darcy."

Darcy's heart thudded.

"There's so much I want to say, but..." His Adam's apple bobbed. "I have so much baggage."

Only the quilt in her arms separated her from him. "I understand about unfinished business, Jax."

The tree house, the swing, the conversation with her father she'd put off for years.

"I don't know how to let go of the past, Darcy. To begin again."

"You don't have to shoulder the weight of the past alone." She lifted her face. "I'm here for you, Jax. If you'll just let me in. Please," she whispered. "Let me in."

Into his heart. Into his life. Into his future.

"Don't you think I want to—" His voice broke. "I long so much for sunshine, baby."

The unexpected endearment turned her insides to mush.

Her heart soared. He felt something for her. She knew he did.

"That last morning before Basic... I never intended to hurt you." He pulled her to his chest, and she dropped the quilt. Her heels came off the ground.

She felt the warmth of his skin, the erratic beat of his heart. He unsettled her in the nicest possible way. It was hard to think, this close to him. She didn't want to think, just wanted to relish this moment.

His chest heaved. He tilted his head. The culmination of her dreams—he was going to kiss her.

In his arms, she didn't feel like the grubby little tomboy who never quite fit in. She felt beautiful and understood and cherished and...

He didn't kiss her.

Instead, he pressed his forehead against hers.

"I'm damaged goods, Darcy. I still have so much to work through before I could ever…"

Whoa. Not what she'd hoped. Was he actually asking her to wait for him? Again? This time, to sort through his feelings for his dead wife?

It felt like she'd already spent most of her life waiting on Jax Pruitt.

More than grief and loneliness stood between them. The tortured guilt he felt over Adrienne's death wasn't something Darcy was prepared to fight.

What was so wrong with her that she always came in second place?

She took herself out of his arms.

"Darcy." His breathing was as rapid as her own. "I owe you so much for what you've done to bring Brody and me together."

Gratitude. Was that what this was with Jax? Some misplaced sense of owing her?

"The rest of the week is booked solid." She struggled to find her footing with him, to return to what they'd always been to each other. "I should go."

Jax nodded.

His easy acceptance of the status quo between them only further tightened the knot in her gut. Why was she so easy to let go of?

"I'll see you tomorrow."

She picked the quilt—and her dignity—off the

sidewalk. "Maybe not. I've decided to join a trekking expedition to Machu Picchu next spring with a group from Alabama. I need to make some calls and finalize my plans."

He stared at her. "The Inca Trail?"

She made herself smile at him. "Come Labor Day, I probably won't be back. For a while."

His shoulders squared. "Right." His mouth flattened.

Anger licked at the underside of her belly. Was that all he could say? Was that all he was going to say?

She was so stupid. A small—or not so small—part of her had wanted him to vehemently protest. To beg her not to go. To ask to go with her.

Idiots didn't come as big or as fanciful as Darcy Parks.

Something flared in his eyes. "Good night then."

Her stomach quivered, treacherously. "Goodbye, Jax." She pivoted.

"That's always been my problem, Darce."

She stopped, her back to him.

"I don't know how to say goodbye to you," he rasped. "Then or now."

She stared straight ahead. Her house was dark, her parents already in bed. "When you figure it out, Jax, let me know."

Leaving him standing alone on the pavement,

she headed up the driveway toward the backyard. Thankful for the darkness, hiding the flow of tears on her cheeks. After all, PKs weren't supposed to cry.

And quietly, she climbed into the tree house.

Chapter Thirteen

Jaxon Pruitt was the biggest idiot that ever lived. If he'd doubted it before, now he knew it to be true. He had a month of lonely days to prove it, too.

No more picnics. No more excursions. No more anything with Darcy.

She was aloof and reserved, keeping her distance. The oh-so-polite, arm's-length smile at the shop. The PK smile she handed him at church every Sunday—a smile she'd never used for him. Until now.

He'd once believed himself a highly trained operative. But Darcy Parks was a genius at evasion. Gliding as effortlessly past his attempts to engage her in conversation as she glided a kayak through a tidal marsh.

Jax had no doubt she'd have probably made a better Green Beret than him. And he was getting very little sleep. Lying in bed, thinking of her while evening thunderstorms boomed overhead.

He was so frustrated with her. Jax raked a hand over his face. Frustrated with himself. Bottom line, he missed her. He missed her more than he'd believed possible, considering he saw her every day. But she wasn't herself with him anymore.

She made sure Brody didn't miss her—Jax would give her that. As hot July mornings turned into even hotter August afternoons, he sweated and guided the business, while she spent lots of time with his son. Long Johns at the diner. Ice cream at the creamery. Having fun—without him.

And he was sick and tired of being without her. He missed teasing her. Horsing around. On the dock, flicking towels at each other. Talking and seeing her eyes brighten. The play of the sunlight across her face. The freckles dancing across the bridge of her nose. He'd lost the sunshine.

Growling, Jax beat his head against the wall behind the counter. What was wrong with him?

"You okay, boss?"

He straightened at Savannah's concern. He pushed off from the wall. "Fine. Never better."

Jax walked outside, scanning the square. Yep, there she was. Pushing Brody on the swing set in the church playground. Having tremendous fun together. And she never even glanced his way.

Instead of this unaccountable pity party, he ought to be glad, grateful Darcy had pulled the plug before they got in over their heads with each other. Sailed past the point of no return.

The night of the Fourth, he'd almost given in to the feelings building within him. The need to tell her—

He blew out a breath. Being unable to completely let her go wasn't fair. They couldn't go on this way. With him pushing her away and reeling her back over and over again. She was smart to walk away from the giant failure that was Jaxon Pruitt.

Yet his reasoning failed to ease the hole in his heart.

Every stinking day when he brought Brody to his mom's, like an idiot, he'd stand on the deck, gazing at the tree house, wondering if Darcy was there. So close and so out of his reach.

Which was as it should be. *Right, God?*

Ironic that what he so feared, he longed for the most. With Darcy, he felt an emotional intimacy he'd never managed to achieve during his marriage to Adrienne. Only increasing his sense of guilt. A never-ending cycle of recrimination.

Why was it so hard to let go of Darcy?

It also bothered him how quickly she'd reverted to what they'd always been to each other. And the idea of her heading across the bridge, hiking the Andes without him…

The prospect—the likelihood—that she'd never return made Jax physically sick to his stomach.

But she was right to steer clear of him. He was a disaster. And if he ever gave in to these impossible feelings for her, they were another disaster in the making. Though if that were true, why did losing her forever cut so deeply?

"Oh, Darce…" he whispered. "What am I going to do with you?" He pinched his nostrils. "What am I ever going to do without you?"

What was wrong with him? He shut his eyes against the obvious answer. Which, because of his situation, was no answer at all.

"Daddy sick?"

He opened his eyes to find Brody standing at the bottom of the shop porch. He raised his gaze. Darcy stood behind his son. He flushed.

Worry pinched Brody's features. "Daddy?"

"Is something wrong, Jax?" She glanced toward the storefront. "Has something happened?"

He swallowed. "Nothing's happened."

Except everything he believed he knew about himself, about her—about him and her—had turned on its head.

She took a step. "Are you all right?" Her voice was sharp.

He scrubbed his hand over his face. "I needed a break."

"Are you sure?" She always read him so well.

He lifted his shoulder and let it drop. "What could be wrong with Jax Pruitt?"

Her eyebrow arched. "Shall I make a list?"

She took Brody's hand and walked him up the steps until they stood next to Jax. "You wanted this business. I'm leaving in two weeks. So you need to stop scaring your son and just suck it up, Pruitt."

He placed his hand over his heart, feigning pain. "Good thing you didn't become a nurse, Darcy. 'Cause you have a terrible bedside manner."

"You seemed glad enough of my bedside manner the time you had your head stuck in a toilet."

Jax laughed. "I did, didn't I?" It felt so good to laugh with her.

Her lips quirked. She never could stay mad at him for long. He'd make sure of it.

"Don't you have an excursion to guide, Jax?"

"Aye, aye, Captain Bligh." He winked at her, intending to annoy. It did.

She rolled her eyes.

"Mc. Mc. Me." Brody bounced in his baby Crocs.

Jax shook his head. "You're not big enough, son. But one day for sure."

Brody poked his lip out and glared. "Me big. Not baby."

Darcy threw Jax a look. "Of course you're not a baby, Brode. Maybe Daddy could bring you back a treasure, though."

"Tweh-zuh?"

"Watch my mouth, Brody." Jax pursed his lips to trill out the consonants. "Tah."

Brody fastened his gaze on his father's lips, concentrating. "Tah."

"Rah."

"Rah," Brody parroted.

"Treasure."

Brody gave a little nod. "Tweh-zuh." He smiled.

Jax sighed.

"Close enough." Darcy ran her hand over his son's silken locks. "Let him be two, Jax. Give him time."

Brody held up three fingers. "Me thwee, Dawcy."

"Not yet, buddy." Jax ruffled his son's hair and as he did so, his hand brushed Darcy's fingers.

Brody leaned into the touch of both their hands. Jax's eyes shot to Darcy.

She took a breath. "Time."

Exactly what he was running out of with her. Already he felt the clock ticking toward her departure. As inexorable and unstoppable as the tide. Leaving him with a vague sense of panic, of impending doom.

But per his usual genius, he came up with a plan. An end run around her defenses.

"Remember how every August 13 we piled into the tree house to watch the Perseid meteor showers?"

Her eyes narrowed. "So?"

"So Brody's never seen a meteor."

"And your point?"

He gave her a supercilious smile. "My point is, today is August 13."

Darcy would have made a good schoolteacher, with her pursed lips and disapproving glare. Though if any of his teachers had looked like her, school would've held a great deal more appeal for him. He folded his arms across his chest.

Her eyes flickered at his movement. "Best viewing won't come till the wee hours of the morning. Kind of late for a little guy like Brody."

"My little guy will be great. We'll bunk tonight at Mom's, and I'll carry him over in time for the show."

"You've thought of everything, haven't you?"

He grinned. "Always do."

"Fine." She sniffed. "Be sure to invite the rest of your tribe."

He rested his shoulder against the porch column. Just 'cause he could—and was rewarded when she scowled at him. Anything was better than her studied indifference of the last month. "You mean my crew?"

"Whatever, Pruitt." She held out her hand to his son. "We only stopped by because Brody wanted to say hello. I told your mom I'd watch him until her hair appointment was finished."

"I look forward to tonight then, Darce."

"That would make one of us, Jax."

But he could tell by the twitching of her lips

she didn't mean it. Darcy, more than anyone else on the planet, was always up for stargazing in the tree house.

And as she walked away with his son, he decided he'd make sure everyone in his family had something else to do tonight.

Leaving him and their toddler-sized chaperone alone in the tree house, to enjoy the meteors with Darcy.

His heart skipped a beat.

Jax kept a tight grip on his son as Brody hurtled past the lower platform to the top of the tree house.

"Dawcy! Dawcy?"

"Not so loud, Brody," he hissed, as the boy stomped up the stairs. "Grandma and Grandpa are sleeping. Miss Agnes and Reverend Harold, too." Not to mention the entire population of seaside Kiptohanock.

Darcy leaned over the railing and waved. "Hey, Brody, honey. I'm so glad you're here."

Was she as glad to see Jax as he was to see her?

Brody, as usual, went for her knees. Bracing for impact, she leaned to hug his son. "I see you dressed for the occasion."

She gently tickled Brody's pajama-clad belly. "I love those gummy bear jammies. Yum. Yum." She grinned at him. "You are such a yummy, gummy jelly bear."

Clasping hands, they did a funny dance, their arms linked.

A dance known only to them. A dance they'd obviously done before. Every time Jax saw Darcy with his son, his heart swelled. And he got crazy ideas about how she'd look carrying his child in her belly one day.

He sucked in a breath. Where had that—?

What was happening here? What was going on with him? Whatever it was, Jax couldn't let it happen.

He glanced around the tree house. This had been a mistake. He shouldn't have invited himself over. He should've never brought Darcy into their lives. He shouldn't have returned to Kiptohanock. *What have I done?* His heart beat at a furious clip.

Jax would've turned and marched down the stairs—if he could have peeled his son off Darcy. No chance of that. Chest aching, he tried breathing in through his nose and out through his mouth. He'd look a right fool if he hyperventilated and keeled over in front of her. He clutched the railing.

Why was he always such an idiot when it came to Darcy? He wasn't about to admit to anything other than an intense attraction. He shut his eyes and tried counting to ten. But these feelings— whatever they were—were going to be the death of him.

She was going to be the death of him. Somehow, somewhere inside, he'd always known that.

Since the long-ago day his mother had sent him to invite Darcy over for freezer pops.

Jax was going to die. He realized it now. A painful, slow, agonizing death, if he didn't get out of here right this—

"Did you climb the steps too fast, Jax?"

His eyes opened.

"Used not to bother you." She smirked. "You must be getting old."

Jax *was* old. An old, washed-up man who loved— No. Absolutely not.

He reached for his son, but instead, her fingers interlocked with his. Something zinged from her fingertips, up his arm and into his chest. A jolt of electricity. He broke out into a sweat.

This must be what it felt like to go into cardiac arrest. He needed to calm down and catch his breath. *Breathe in the breath of God... Breathe out the breath of life.* He could still make it to the truck if he—

She tugged him toward one of the red lawn chairs she kept stashed there. "I brought treats for while we wait."

He fell into a chair. She was a treat in her hip-hugging, cuffed jeans. He sighed. *I'm not making it out of here alive, am I, God?*

Easing into the adjacent chair, she smiled at him. Not feeling constrained, Brody plopped himself into her lap. And she proceeded to hand-feed his Cubby Bear of a boy cheese puffs.

"Don't tell Grandma Gail," she whispered. "But I figure it's a special occasion, and a little junk food never hurt anyone, right?"

"Right," Jax whispered back in a hoarse, conspiratorial voice.

A tendril of strawberry blonde hair fell over Darcy's face as she bent over his son.

Jax curled his twitching fingers around the underside of the armrests for safekeeping.

This was why he hadn't had the courage to come to the tree house the day he reported for Basic. Because if he had... If he had...

He wrenched his gaze from the delicate curve of her cheek to the circle of night sky in the tree canopy overhead. A luminous streak of neon green flashed through the black velvet of the night.

"Look, Brody." She pointed.

Brody's eyes grew round as sand dollars. Jax, however, couldn't take his eyes off the woman holding his son. As the heavens rained glory, somehow it felt to Jax as if it was for their wonderment alone.

On this night. In this tree house. With Darcy Parks, tomboy next door. His sister's BFF. The sword-clashing PK extraordinaire, who'd managed to bring his hurting son out of his shell and bridge the gap to his father.

A woman who made Jax forget who he was, what he'd been and what he'd done. Making him long for a thousand nights like this. Yearning to be the man Darcy deserved. Failing and yet…

He turned toward the shooting stars burning through the darkness overhead. A comfortable silence fell as they waited through a lull for another celestial light show.

A sea breeze ruffled the leaves on the branches around them.

"I can give you my shirt if you're cold, Darce."

She laughed, low in her throat. "I've got your son to keep me warm, Jax."

He glanced over, to find Brody's arms entwined around her shoulders. His head was tucked into the sweet curve of her neck, his eyes closed shut. His gentle breaths rose and fell.

The ache in Jax's gut intensified.

"I could watch Brody sleep all night." A strand of hair fell over her eyes.

And Jax could no more fight the what-ifs, the what-should've-beens, the what-could-bes than he could stop himself from taking his next breath.

Coming out of the chair, he crouched beside Darcy. Her eyes widened. And giving in to an urge he'd felt surely since the dawn of time, he touched a tendril of her hair.

Wrapped his finger in its silken softness. Held it to his lips, inhaling the tantalizing scent of citrus. Coconut and papaya. Darcy…

"Jax?"

"This," he whispered. "This is why I didn't

come that morning. Heading off to war, this is what I wanted most to do and yet I couldn't tell you, Darcy..." He heaved a breath.

Darcy lifted her hand, hesitated, then placed it against his cheek. He leaned closer. Her eyes became luminous.

At last. Finally. He—

Sitting up suddenly in Darcy's lap, Brody broke them apart. "Me sweepy, Daddy. Go home." He rubbed his eyes with his fists.

Darcy sagged in the chair. Jax slumped. Her eyes filled—with relief or regret?

He stood, not sure he could trust his legs, and took hold of his son. "We're having a sleepover at Grandma's tonight, remember, Brode?"

Cradling his son against his chest, he turned at the top of the steps. "We're not done here, Darcy."

"I don't know what you mean."

"I think you do."

She crossed her arms.

"You and I have unfinished business."

"Do we?" She lifted her chin. "Before I leave, you mean?"

Yes, they did. Neither one of them could go on this way. He knew he surely couldn't.

"I'll see you here in the morning, Darce."

She scowled at him. "What makes you think I'll be here, Jaxon Pruitt?"

"Because I know you, Darcy Parks, and that's where you are every morning." He looked at her. "And this time, this is a promise I aim to keep."

Chapter Fourteen

Early the next morning, Darcy sat alone once more in the top of the tree house, her upturned face soaking in the dappled sunshine. Talking to God.

It had been painful staying away from Jax over the last month. Going out of her way to avoid him. Seeing the conflict, hurt and confusion in his eyes.

Her stomach went topsy-turvy, remembering Jax with Brody during last night's meteor shower. Was there anything sweeter than a strong man holding a child in his arms?

She was jarred from her musing—okay, her mooning—by a heavy tread on the steps. He'd kept his word.

He was here. Was he finally starting to feel for her what she felt for him? Getting out of her chair, Darcy felt delicious anticipation curl in her belly.

"Long time no see, soldier."

He stopped on the landing. "Permission to come aboard?"

She smirked. "At your peril, Jax."

After a lonely July, their banter felt good. Comforting. Like slipping into a pair of well-worn and well-loved jeans.

Feet planted at hip's width, he smiled at her in that half-lidded, ridiculously stomach-quivering way of his. She took a step back, hand to her throat.

His smile slipped, but his dark eyes smoldered. "I've been thinking about where we went wrong."

She bit her lip. "There's never been a 'we,' Jax."

"Maybe that was our mistake. Maybe we should've just gotten it out of our system." His gaze reduced her to a quivery mass of emotional gelatin.

She tried to get a grip on her nerves. "Last time you said that to me, you asked me to punch you."

He took a step toward her. And she took another step back, feeling the need to insert a breath of distance between them. Tree bark scraped against her shirt.

"This time I had something different in mind." He moved closer. "Perhaps back then we should've just locked lips and moved on." His face, his mouth, were tantalizingly near.

Maybe she hadn't heard him right. "A kiss?"

She was having a hard time breathing. "You want to kiss me?"

"Why not? Otherwise, we'll always wonder."

Her heart hammered. She fought the tidal pull of his gaze. "How about let's just chalk it up to misplaced pheromones?" Better to play off his flippant words.

"Chemistry. Electricity. Whatever you want to call it, it is something, Darce. Always has been. This thing between us."

"While some women might be bowled over by the sheer humility of your offer, thanks but no thanks." She pushed at his chest. "I've survived this long without Jaxon Pruitt. I think I'm good for another few decades." This wasn't how she'd envisioned this morning unfolding.

He braced his hand on the tree trunk beside her head. "Here's the thing, though. Not sure I want to go the next few decades without knowing. I've spent way too long thinking, wondering…"

She blinked. Jax had thought about her? Wondered about her and him… Could it be true? Did he feel the same way for her that she felt about him?

Why was she fighting him? When all her life, she'd wanted him to kiss her. She was leaving in a few weeks. And she'd missed spending time with him. Why not? Why not just this once?

His brow constricted, he searched her face.

Unable to bear the exquisite tension between them any longer, she stretched on her tiptoes toward him. Grasped hold of his broad shoulders, lest like last time, somehow this moment moved beyond her reach.

His fingers found their way into the long strands of her hair. "Darcy…" His hands cupped the crown of her head.

Closing his eyes, he touched his lips to her mouth. Incredible sweetness. An incredible rightness.

Better than Mondays. Better than lime-green freezer pops. Better than anything she ever dared dream. Though her dreams had always been full of him. Jax holding her in his strong arms. Jax kissing her.

If she died right now here at the tree house— their tree house—she'd never want anything more. He crushed her against his chest. Then suddenly he yanked his mouth from hers.

Leaving her struggling to make sense of it all.

He pressed his forehead against hers. "Now we know." His thumb traced the line of her cheek.

"Now we know."

She felt like singing. She felt like dancing. She felt like she'd plunged out of an airplane without a parachute. Not a bad analogy when it came to life with Jax.

"Good thing we checked." She laughed "Electricity for real. Chemistry for sure." So worth the wait.

He didn't laugh. The teasing light in his eyes had gone. He took a step backward and let go of her.

She frowned, sensing more than a physical withdrawal.

He combed his fingers across his head. "I shouldn't have kissed you. Not with how things are with me. Not with you leaving soon."

What was wrong? Didn't he see how wonderful they were together? Couldn't he see the beautiful future she glimpsed when they were in each other's arms?

"I don't have to go, Jax. I—"

"So I guess that's that." He dropped his eyes to the platform. "I appreciate everything you've done this summer for me and Brody. Your patience in teaching me the business. Your friendship."

She flinched.

Was that what this was? An experiment? Like he said, something to get out of their systems? And now that he'd kissed her, was he done with her?

Because one kiss didn't get him out of Darcy's system. One kiss only made her long for more. For forever.

Surely Jax couldn't have kissed her like that unless he loved her, too. Could he? Apparently, he could. He was Jaxon Pruitt, after all.

How for one stolen moment could she have forgotten? He was a man with far more experience than she. The kind of man who'd had his pick of women. Who'd married a gorgeous woman like Adrienne Maserelli.

Worse yet, how could Darcy have forgotten who she was? The gauche PK. A hateful blush crept from beneath the neckline of her shirt.

"You're leaving in a few weeks. Brody and I are setting down roots here. You'll meet some Floridian guy…"

"I don't want some Floridian guy, Jax."

He took a giant step backward, and pressed against the railing. "Don't say that, Darcy."

Why did something hold Jax back from pursuing a relationship with her? Or maybe she was deluding herself. Again.

Maybe everything between them was merely a product of her pathetic imagination.

"It's best not to risk our friendship, Darce."

She gave a hoarse laugh. "Somehow, Jaxon, I thought we were beyond that."

"I'm not what you need, Darcy."

"What about what I want? What do *you* want, Jax?"

She was losing him. All they'd shared. All they were to each other. Before they ever had a chance to become more.

"You make me want things I can never have, but wanting isn't enough, Darcy. Eventually, you'd hate me. And hurting you isn't something I can bear."

Was it guilt that truly held Jax in an unyielding stranglehold? Or a love for his dead wife so abiding he'd made a grave of his heart?

"After Adrienne..." He scoured his neck with his hand. "I can't go there with you, Darcy. I just can't."

Darcy's cheeks burned. She must've been crazy to think she could follow a woman like that in Jax's life.

She was so stupid. Stupid to think that she could ever be more than a runner-up for someone like Jax. Stupid to hope. Stupid to dream he'd ever love her.

Darcy closed her eyes. Brody needed a mother even if Jax didn't think he needed a wife. Brody was his Achilles' heel. She fought the urge to convince Jax to let her love them. To make life better for them both.

The insidious fear of how easily she could persuade Jax shook Darcy. And at how little she was willing to settle for if it meant keeping them in her life.

She knew if she didn't get away from him right this minute, she'd humiliate herself by begging him for a place in his life at any cost. Even if it meant being yet again second best. Satisfied for any crumbs of affection he deigned to toss her way.

Kind of what she'd done all summer? Her entire life? She was such an idiot. Such a history-repeats-itself little idiot.

Someday he'd get over Adrienne. Or maybe he wouldn't. But she couldn't stick around to find out. Because if he did manage to put the past behind him, he'd still never choose her.

Rigid with strain, Darcy pulled herself together. "Guess you found a way to say goodbye, after all."

"Trust me, this is for the best."

"Trust you?" She must've been certifiable to ever trust him again. To ever let him back into her life.

He flushed. "I realize it's hard to understand, but Darce—"

"Don't call me that," she growled. "You don't get to kiss me, reject me and then still call me that."

"I never meant to hurt—"

"You never mean to do anything, do you?" She shoved his chest with the palm of her hand. "You need to leave, Jaxon."

He staggered. "I'm sorry, Darcy. So, so sorry."

The last tether on her self-control, her pride, snapped. Like a hot air balloon rising toward the sky.

"Just go," she yelled. "I don't ever want to see you again, Jaxon. Not ever."

"What's going on up there?" Her father stood at the base of the tree. He wouldn't come up. He never did.

Mouth tight, Jax shouldered past her dad.

Down below, the screen door banged. "Darcy?"

She squeezed her eyes shut. Not Mom, too. Darcy's life, as always, was a public spectacle.

Hands on her hips, her mother stood on the porch steps. "What's going on?"

In the distance, she heard the unmistakable sound of Jax's truck. Her lips flattened. Leaving—something Jaxon Pruitt had mastered. She slumped over the railing.

"Darcy?" She'd never heard her father's voice sound so sharp. "What's wrong, honey?"

"What were you thinking, bellowing at Jaxon like that?" Her mother joined him at the foot of the oak. "Half of the Kiptohanock grapevine is probably on the phone with the other half right now."

"Let them talk." She tromped down to the first platform. "I'm done with being good ole, get-along, go-along Darcy."

"I don't like your tone," her mother huffed. "Have you forgotten who you are, Darcy Parks?"

Her father's brows bunched, a thundercloud on his face. "What did Jaxon do to you?"

Was that concern—for her—on his face?

"Must we do this out here?" Her mother heaved a sigh. "Let's go inside, and talk about what has you in such a stir."

"I resign." Darcy flounced—she who had never flounced in her life—down the remaining steps to ground level. "I'm done being the PK around here."

Her mother gave her an exasperated glance. "This drama is unlike you, Darcy. At this time of the morning…when your father has an appointment—"

Suddenly, Darcy just lost it. "Dad has an appointment with a cemetery, Mother. And I'm done with all of it," she shouted.

Her parents both took an inadvertent step back. Next door, the Pruitts must think she'd lost her mind.

"What do you mean?" Her mother's face creased. "Done with what?"

Darcy threw out her arms. "Blame it on my hair. Blame it on a thousand days that end in *y*. I'm sick of being runner-up to everybody within shouting distance of this tree."

Her mother's gaze flickered toward Darcy's father. "I really don't think now is the time or—"

"I hate this tree!" She pounded her fist against the trunk. "Where second choice for me began before I was ever born."

Her mother tapped her foot on the ground. "You don't hate this tree, Darcy."

"I hate it. I do." She jutted her chin. "I love it and I hate it. Like I love the brother I never met, Dad. Maybe I hate him, too. Or maybe I just hate the aching hole he left in your heart."

Her father flinched.

"You're upsetting your father." Her mom inserted her arm in the crook of his elbow. "We don't talk about—"

Darcy continued as if she hadn't spoken. "A hole I've tried—unsuccessfully—to fill my entire life. But I can't. It's time I accepted that, and got over it."

Her mother straightened. "I cannot believe you're acting like this, Darcy Rose Parks. After what your father's been through—"

"I give up, Mother." She threw out her hands. "I give up trying. I'm giving up this tree." She cut her eyes to the Pruitt house. "I'm giving up lime-green freezer pops and Kiptohanock. For good."

Her mother bristled. "You're making no sense."

"I'm sorry to be such a disappointment to you, but I'm climbing the Inca Trail to Machu Picchu, Mom."

"Disappointment? What are you talking about?" Her mother's lips thinned. "What has gotten into you, Darcy?"

"I'm going to kayak a stretch of the Amazon. I'm going to windsurf off the North Shore of Hawaii." She glared at the Pruitt house. "With or without someone to climb, paddle or surf alongside me."

Her father just stood there.

"Why do you never see me?" Something inside Darcy cracked and broke. "I'm going to seize my dreams, Dad. I can't be Colin. I can't live the life he might've had."

Her mother's mouth wobbled. "Don't, Darcy."

But Darcy had eyes only for her father. "I can't keep hoping that one day you'll choose me and love me the way you love him."

Her mother's face flamed. "Please, Darcy..."

She sucked in a breath, the reason she'd never left home suddenly crystal clear for the first time in her life. "I can't be the child who never leaves you, Dad, just because Colin did."

Her father reeled as if from a blow.

Tears cascaded from her mother's eyes. "How could you, Darcy?"

Looking older than she'd ever seen him, her father freed himself from her mother's grasp. "We should've talked about Colin and Linda a long time ago."

This time, her mother winced. "Harold..."

"She's right." Her father's face crumpled. "I used my work as a distraction, an excuse. But I never meant to hurt either of you," he whispered.

"Your life with him was always enclosed in this glass jar, untouchable, out of reach. And we were on the outside, looking in, Dad."

Her mother shook her head. "Your father has been very open about his struggles."

A vulnerability that endeared him to so many hurting people.

Darcy bit her lip. "With everyone but us."

His face constricted. "I never meant to shut you out, Darcy. I didn't want to cloud the wonderful second-chance life I'd been given with you and your mom with the dark grief I carried."

"Were we your second chance, Dad?" she whispered. "Or second choice? Why did everything belong to him?"

Bubbling out from the deepest places in her heart, she found the words she'd yearned to express but had dared not for fear of losing what little of her father was hers.

"Did you not save anything of yourself for me?" She gestured at the tree house. "Was there no place left in your heart just for me? For us?"

"The swing was yours," her mother rasped. "Your father put the swing there for you, Darcy."

Darcy gaped at them. "The swing wasn't part of the original tree house?"

"The swing was ours alone." Her father sighed. "But one day, you just stopped. You wouldn't swing anymore."

"When I found the carved initials... I assumed..." She choked back a sob.

"I'm so sorry, Darcy." Her father touched her shoulder. "For ever making you feel second best. Forgive me, please."

There'd been so much pain. For each of them.

"It's time for there to be only honesty between us." He gripped the railing. "Colin and Linda were killed on a Monday."

"Dad, you don't have to—"

"Colin needed a new pair of shoes from the mall

in Salisbury. But a parishioner called." He gave them a wan smile. "I've always been a workaholic. Struggled with false pride. It could've waited for another day. Instead, I sent Linda and Colin off without me. I should've died with them that day."

Weeping, her mother sat down heavily on the step. "I'm glad you didn't die."

"So am I." Taking her mother's hand, he lifted it to his lips. "Because if I'd died, I would've never had the opportunity to love you, Agnes."

Her mother's chin quivered. Darcy had never seen her parents so tender with each other.

"I didn't stop to think how being a preacher's kid might make you feel. Forgive me, too." Her mother touched Darcy's cheek. "No more PK."

Darcy blinked away tears.

Her father enfolded Darcy in his arms. "As my beloved daughter, you have a place all your own in my life. And if God has created a desire in your heart to kayak the Amazon, you'll carry my love wherever God leads you."

"Really, Dad?" Something inside her seemed to rise, floating above the treetops.

He exhaled a long, slow breath. "It's August 14. And I'd like to tell you both about Linda and Colin. Not keep it bottled inside anymore." He swallowed. "Would you come to the cemetery with me?"

"I'd like that, Harold." Agnes pressed her cheek against his sleeve. "To share not just the joy, but the sorrow, too." And shining in her mother's features was a newfound confidence, a security in his love.

"Darcy?"

In his eyes, she glimpsed the truth of his heart. Her father loved her. She could see it now. Despite his pain, he'd always loved her.

"Whatever the future holds, Dad—" her voice hitched "—we'll share it together."

The past with its pain and sorrow could never be erased. It was part of him. In truth, it had made him into the caring man—pastor, husband and father—she loved. It was time to stop fighting her father's past. But to accept it and help him shoulder the weight of it.

"But first…" She bit her lip. "Would you push me in the swing again, Dad?"

A smile lifted his cheeks. "I'd like that, Darcy. So much."

Sitting on the wooden slat, she coiled her hands around the chains. Her feet no longer dangled.

"Ready, honey?"

She glanced over her shoulder. A warmth filled his face.

"Yes, Daddy. I am."

"Off you go then." After pulling on the chains, he let go. Her feet left the ground as she sailed forward. "Higher, Dad. Make it go higher."

Faster and faster. She pumped her legs. Her

father's gentle prodding propelled her upward and onward.

Darcy closed her eyes. In the swing, she broke the laws of gravity. She could fly. Bunching her muscles, she gathered strength and soared into the wild blue yonder.

Free and light. Higher and higher. Until the years and the cares dropped away. Until the sunlight danced across her cheeks, the wind whistling past.

Her mother and father laughed, their heads close together. The swing slowed. She no longer strained to reach the heights, content to let gravity hold her in its sway. Satisfied to have her feet touch the ground. To rejoin the ones she loved and who loved her.

"Bravo, Darcy!" Her father's eyes grew misty. "Bravo, my beautiful, adventurous girl."

Coming out of the swing, she wrapped her arms around his stout waist. "I'm a swing kind of girl, Daddy," she whispered against his shirt.

"I'm a swing kind of dad, Darcy." His voice was choked with unshed tears. "I love you, honey."

And though it wasn't Monday, her dad took the day off. They talked about many things. So many misunderstandings were erased.

But it was at the cemetery, standing beside her father, that she began to truly fathom how heavy was the burden of guilt. And in light of the Father's promises, how unnecessary.

She ached for the wreckage guilt had brought to Jax's heart. How she wished he could know how it felt to be free and light. No longer weighed down by the past and his failures.

Help Jax, God. Show him how much You love him.

A disquieting notion floated across her consciousness, like the tang of sea salt on the breeze. And she sensed that now was not the time to go to Florida. Not yet. That perhaps she needed to stay on the Shore, if just for a little while longer.

No matter the cost to her own heart, she must be there for Jax and Brody. To be their burdensharer. With no agenda or expectations of her own. Except to help Jax accept the past, embrace the present and move on into the future.

God would reveal to her when it was time for her to leave. She could entrust her life and her plans into His hands. The safest place they could be. A peace, too long denied, flooded her being.

Florida. Her dreams. Machu Picchu would wait.

Jax and his grieving heart could not.

Chapter Fifteen

At the distant rumble of thunder that afternoon, Jax shut off the kitchen faucet. His gaze automatically darted to the backyard, where Brody was playing. But he wasn't there.

Jax's heart missed a beat. His son was probably running his trucks in the sand underneath the deck. "Brody?"

But when he'd clambered down the steps, a quick scan revealed no little boy. "Brody! Answer Daddy, please." Also missing was the red dump truck.

One minute he'd been there and the next, he was gone. How far could a toddler go? The answer—too far, too fast. Sweat having nothing to do with August humidity broke out on Jax's forehead.

Hands on his hips, he scoped the terrain, assessing the risks. The creek—

Jax took off at a run. Brody knew better than to

go to the water without an adult. But kids didn't think about danger.

He reached the shoreline out of breath. His personal kayaks remained tied well out of the reach of the tide. But no little guy. If Brody wasn't down here, where was he?

Thunder clapped, closer than before. Rumbling like a kettledrum, fixing to blow a gale, as the old-timers would say. And like the born here he was, he immediately panned his gaze over the salt marsh in the direction of the barrier islands. Low, roiling greenish clouds eclipsed the sun's rays.

He shivered at the abrupt drop in temperature. "Brody!" His voice had gone rough with fear. There was a heavy intensity to the unnatural stillness of the air.

Maybe Brody had gone inside the house, slipping past him. Unlikely, but Jax tore across the lawn once more. Clattering up the wooden steps, he yanked open the French doors. Inside, he lunged for the staircase. "Brody? Where are you, son?"

But except for the hum of the refrigerator and the whir of the air conditioning, only silence greeted him.

Adrenaline pumping through his veins, he did a complete, aimless three-sixty. Fear seized his heart. Where was Brody? What had happened to him?

Jerking at the sound of tires crunching gravel,

Jax raced for the stairs. Someone was here. Had someone taken Brody? Were they even now taking his son away from him forever?

His emotions seesawing, Jax hurtled toward the front door. On the porch, he came to a sudden halt as Darcy stepped out of her SUV. The last person he'd ever expected to see again.

Gasping for breath, he bent over, hands on his knees. His chest felt tight and he could smell the coming rain.

"Jax? What's wrong?"

"It's Brody. He's gone." He squeezed his eyes shut. "I can't find him anywhere."

Darcy had taken one look at his blanched face and known something was terribly wrong.

As if unable to support his own weight, Jax listed heavily against the porch column. She'd come out here to apologize for screaming at him. To ask his forgiveness and for permission to be a continuing part of their lives as a friend. But now?

The wind picked up speed, blowing tendrils of hair across her face.

She brushed the strands out of her eyes. "What happened? Where was he when you last saw him? How long has he been missing?"

"Fifteen minutes, but it feels like longer. He was right outside the window. I took my eyes off him for one second..."

"This isn't your fault, Jax."

His terror for Brody radiated in palpable waves, the primal terror of every parent whose child has ever wandered away in a store. And because of her deep connection to the little boy, she fought against the horror threatening to engulf her, as well.

This wasn't the time to fall apart. She needed to think calmly. Clearly. "He's not been gone that long." She gripped Jax's upper arm. "Where have you checked?"

"I ran down to the creek first thing, but it didn't look as if he'd been there. So I searched the house next, but no Brody." His breath came in ragged spurts. "Where could he be?"

"We'll find him, Jax." He shook like a beech tree in a winter squall. "I'll help you look."

Jax gripped her hand so hard, she winced. But she held on to him.

"He knows better than to wander off, Darcy."

"Brody is a curious two-year-old boy. Something could have caught his attention—a bird or a butterfly—and he followed it into the woods."

"Darcy, we're surrounded by woods on every side. Isolated out here. No other house for miles." Jax's eyes widened. "Suppose he isn't in the woods? Suppose somebody…"

"Worst case scenario, but there's no time to lose." She dug out her phone. "I'm calling for help." She hit 911. "Do you have your phone on you?"

He fished it out of his jeans.

"Call my dad. He'll get a group together to help us look. Hello…" She pointed her mouth at the receiver. "This is an emergency." She relayed the situation to the dispatcher.

Moments later, she clicked off. "They're sending a patrol car and issuing an Amber Alert."

"If someone's taken Brody, he could be anywhere by now. Scared. Hurt—"

"Don't go there, Jax. We don't have enough information. The Amber Alert will have law enforcement on the lookout."

She pulled him close. His heartbeat thumped in his chest. "For once, small town nosiness could come in handy."

He swallowed. "I talked to your dad. He and Seth Duer plus a bunch of other people are on their way. Thank God you came when you did." His mouth twisted. "So much for my training. I was losing it."

The look in his eyes turned her heart inside out. "You're entitled to lose it. He's not some mission. He's your son."

Darcy wrapped her arms around Jax. He was so scared. "I won't leave you until we find Brody."

"There's a storm brewing. What if—"

She stepped back. "No what-ifs. We'll do what's in our power to do, and we won't stop looking until we find him."

"You're right." He scrubbed his neck with his hand. "And if I've learned nothing else, we must pray for God to watch over Brody, keep him safe and lead us to him."

She tugged at his hand. "Let's try the woods."

Only a few yards in, the forest closed around them, darker, gloomier than the billowing clouds looming over the marsh. Leaves carpeted the ground.

The thick air was saturated with a musky, earthy scent. Beads of perspiration trickled between Darcy's shoulder blades, leaving her shirt clinging to her back. The heat was stifling.

She batted away a swarm of gnats. A strange sense of heaviness hung in the air, covering her like a shroud. It felt as if the world was waiting for something to happen...

First, plinking sounds, as raindrops bounced off the leaves of the trees. Feeling cold against her skin. The precipitation became more rapid.

She plunged deeper into the woods after Jax, following his lead without question. It was far too easy to become disoriented inside the forest, with familiar landmarks like the sky and water obscured. If confusing for them, how much more for Brody? But now was not the time for pessimism.

Jax found the small, red dump truck lying haphazardly among the pine needles.

"We're on the right track. We'll find him soon, Jax."

He exhaled. "I need to stop thinking like a father and start thinking like the tracker I was trained to be. Let's walk ten feet apart. Look for any signs that he passed this way."

She fanned out. "What kind of signs?"

Head bent, he stalked the path with long strides. "A clump of mud. Scuffled leaves. A twisted blade of grass."

Going still, he crouched beside a gulley filled with brackish water. "Here's something."

Seeing the imprint of five little toes, she swallowed. "We're going to find him, Jax. We're getting closer." She kept her eyes fastened on the leaf-strewn deer trail.

They emerged from the shelter of the overhanging tree canopy to the stinging pelt of rain. Lightning flashed. She flinched.

She gasped as the clouds released a deluge upon them, further obscuring their line of sight. Drenching them. Soaking their clothes within minutes.

Darcy shivered. Brody must be so cold and frightened.

Jax grabbed her hand. "Let's try this way."

They plodded on. The rain flowed down their cheeks, stung their eyes. Water filled her mouth every time she called Brody's name.

Above the pounding noise of the torrential rain, their voices grew louder, their calls more frantic.

His hair plastered to his head, Jax caught Darcy's arm when she slipped in the mud. Then stepping over a fallen log, she lost her flip-flop, but didn't bother to stop. Driven by the need to hurry before the storm grew worse, she kicked off the other one. Her bare feet were better for running.

The trail abruptly stopped at the edge of the water. Jax's face paled. A flash flood had carved out a small, tree-covered island midstream. The mighty rush of water whirled, separating them not only from the island, but also blocking them from reaching the rest of the forest.

He lifted his face to the pelting rain. "Show us where to look, God. Help us find Brody. Please."

Whistling, the wind lashed the trees on the small island into violent gyrations. The creek water spilled over its banks, lapping at her feet.

Thunder boomed. They both jolted. Lightning sizzled the air. The hairs on Darcy's arms stood up. An electrical discharge of ozone pinched her nostrils.

Over the wail of the wind, she heard a faint cry. She strained to pinpoint the source of the sound.

Jax's gaze flicked to her. "What?"

At the base of two trees on the island, something yellow moved. Not a color naturally found in the arboreal forest of the maritime Eastern Shore.

"Brody!" she screamed.

"Where?"

She pointed.

"Brody!" Jax yelled, waving his arms. "Brody!"

The child took a step toward the surging water.

"No!" she and Jax shouted simultaneously. "Stay there."

Across the watery divide from them, his little face puckered.

Darcy raised both palms to shoulder height. "Don't get in the water, sweetie. Stay right where you are."

With the cloud-to-ground lightning, he was only marginally safer in the trees. But if he got in the water, he'd be swept away.

"Do what Darcy says, son."

She couldn't tell if the wetness on Brody's cheeks came from tears or the rain. Probably both.

Brody's lips quavered. "Hey, Dawcy."

"Hey, Brody." Her throat closed.

"Daddy is coming to get you, son. Stay where you are." He took a deep breath. "I'll come in the kayak. Okay?"

"It'll take the both of us fighting the current to reach him, Jax."

He raked his fingers through his rain-slicked hair. "I can't let you—"

"Just try and stop me." She glared.

"Okay," he rasped.

His jawline hardened as he raised his voice again. "Brody, we're going to get the kayak, but don't go anywhere. We'll be back quick as we can."

Brody's head bobbed. "'Kay, Daddy. Me wait fow you."

The unquestioning trust in his voice caused Darcy's eyes to brim with tears.

"Daddy's coming. I promise," Jax called across the water.

She hated leaving Brody stranded on the island. But every second counted. They ran as if their lives depended on it. Brody's life did. If anything happened to him…

The loss of a child. Nothing was worse. She couldn't let what had happened to her father happen to Jax. Not if it took every bit of strength she possessed. Not while she still had breath in her body.

Chapter Sixteen

On Jax's heels, she raced through the brambles. Branches slapped her cheeks. Thorns tore at her clothing. She was panting by the time they reached the floating dock on the creek bank.

"We'll take the tandem kayak." His fingers trembled as he wrestled with the knots. "Less stable, but we'll need the extra space for the three of us." He clenched his teeth, his gaze fierce. "Because three of us will be coming home."

The normally placid tidal creek had become a maelstrom of raging currents. They didn't have the proper kayak or gear for conditions resembling white-water rapids. But the clock was ticking. The island could be swamped at any moment by the flash flood.

"I'll get the paddles." She ran to the storage shed.

She grabbed two adult PFDs and Brody's smaller one. She quickly donned and buckled her own life vest. After inserting her hand through the armholes of the other PFDs, she seized two paddles.

Jax had freed the kayak, shoving it to the edge of the water. She held a life vest out to him. He shook his head.

"Put it on, Jax. If we roll, you drowning isn't going to help me rescue Brody."

Grimacing, he strapped on the vest and held the kayak for her to scramble inside. Stuffing Brody's PFD into the space at her feet, she settled into the bow. She stuck her paddle into the creek bed, stabilizing the boat as best she could for Jax.

In one lithe motion, he leaped aboard, and they pushed off. Like a cork bobbing topsy-turvy in the tempestuous current, they battled the water, trying to gain a semblance of control. Lightning crackled, splitting the sky overhead. They maneuvered the kayak around floating debris. Downed branches scraped against the craft.

As lookout, she did her best to identify obstacles in their route and course correct, dodging the rocks in the rushing creek. But there were too many hazards to steer around completely. They banged from one rock to the next like a silver ball in a pinball machine.

They kept the kayak at an angle as they approached a wave. Riding the swell, Darcy laid her paddle across her lap. Once the kayak dropped, they paddled in harmony, broad, strong strokes.

The blades sliced through the water, eating up the distance.

A moment too late, she spotted a submerged boulder portside. "Ten o'clock. Watch—" The kayak tipped at an impossible angle. They threw their weight to the other side, but it was too late.

"Hold on!" Jax yelled.

She reinforced her grip on the paddle, maintaining the set-up position. There was a surreal sensation as the sky tilted and everything went upside down. The water closed over her head, the sudden chill a shock.

But she held on to the paddle and didn't panic. Three seconds was what they practiced. She ticked off the seconds in her head, willing Jax to have recovered enough to implement the plan.

One, two, three, Elvis.

She flicked her hip to the right and reached for the sky. The kayak tipped.

Water streamed off her body and the paddle. Keeping her head tucked, she dared not check on Jax. For a heartbeat, gravity held them in its grip, but then the kayak flipped upright again.

"Darcy…"

"I'm okay!" Hunching, she took up the cadence of the stroke once more. She put the strength of her core into it.

Up ahead, the island appeared. And the familiar, altogether wonderful sight of a little boy in yellow. He waved from the rapidly diminishing beachhead. Darcy and Jax drove the kayak as far up onto the land as they could.

"I'll hold it. You—"

But she was already out of the kayak, the paddle stowed. Their efforts in unison. Thinking alike. One in purpose and plan.

Splashing through the calf-deep water, she reached for Brody, his life jacket threaded on her forearm. He jumped into her arms.

"Dawcy…" He buried his small, cold face into the hollow of her neck.

She got him into the PFD. "This time me do." She snapped the buckles herself. Sweeping him into her arms again, she turned toward the water.

Jax's face was contorted with the effort to keep the kayak from being torn from the beach. "I can't hold it much…" He gritted his teeth.

Placing Brody near the bow, she slipped inside. Once in her seat, she wrapped her legs around Brody's quivering body and took up her paddle.

Shoving off, Jax let the plunging current take them. The paddles were useless now, except to keep the kayak from ricocheting off water hazards and capsizing.

The kayak hurtled downstream. There'd be no chance to pilot it onto Jax's land. There was only one way to exit the out-of-control water ride. Split-second coordination was essential before the flood swept them out to sea.

Glancing over her shoulder, Darcy locked gazes

with Jax. He gave her a barely perceptible nod, but she knew what he was thinking. Because she knew him so well. And he knew her.

Timing, like in life, was everything. They had one chance and only one to get this right the first time. She let go of her paddle. It churned before disappearing beneath the rolling water.

She pulled Brody onto her lap. "Remember how to do a wet exit, Brody?"

His brown eyes large, he nodded.

"I need you to hold on to me and don't let go, monkey boy." She gulped. "No matter what happens, don't let go. Okay?"

He twined his arms around her neck. "'Kay, Dawcy."

She gave Jax a tremulous smile. "We're ready."

"Darcy, I…" He shook the rain out of his eyes. "Later. One…"

"Hold your breath like we practiced, Brody," she whispered into his ear.

Jax let go of his paddle. "Two…"

She tensed.

"Three…"

Hurling themselves out of the kayak, they plunged into the stream. She and Brody sank, the water closing over their heads. The powerful force of the current sucked him out of her arms. She flailed, reaching for something of him to grasp on to.

God… Help—

A small, round head banged into her chest. She found the loop at the back of Brody's PFD.

Never letting go of her grip on him, she scissors kicked and stretched upward. They erupted above the water. Choking, sputtering, she dog-paddled, fighting to keep from being washed farther downstream, where the channel widened.

There was no sign of Jax. Had he become entangled underwater? Her instinct was to scream his name, but she couldn't give in to her fear. She had no time to search for him, with Brody's life at stake.

Rotating the little boy onto his back, she towed him toward shore. He kicked his legs in the water, keeping himself buoyant.

Only when her feet scraped bottom did she realize she'd made it. She hauled Brody out of the water to higher ground, glancing about frantically for Jax.

At the top of the bank, they flopped onto the wet grass, clutching each other. Shaking from more than the cold. She peered through the trees, trying to get her bearings. Maybe they were somewhere near the Savage farm?

Brody's lips puckered. "Daddy?"

She leaped to her feet. If she could spot any sign of him, she'd go back into the water. Brody needed his daddy. She bit back a sob. She needed Brody's daddy.

But there was nothing. Only dark water. The

rain had stopped. As had the thunder and lightning. The storm had moved out to sea.

Was Jax—

She cut off the thought.

Brody clung to her thigh. "Daddy?"

The brush rustled as several men in neon orange burst into the clearing. The volunteer water-rescue team. Ethan and Luke Savage. Sawyer Kole. Weston Clark.

Hoisting Brody into her arms, she stumbled toward them. "Jax's still in the water." There was a rising note of hysteria in her voice. "You have to find him."

The radio on Luke Savage's shoulder crackled. He paused as the other men swept toward her. Weston pulled off his jacket, draping it around her and Brody.

But she shrugged out of his coat, brushing aside his attempt to take the little boy from her. Brody whimpered, tightening his legs around her torso.

She'd fight them if she had to. She wasn't letting go of Brody, and she wasn't going to let them stand here doing nothing while Jax drowned.

They had to do something now. Before it was too late. If it wasn't already too late. Nausea roiled in her stomach.

"I'm fine. We're fine. But not Jax. You have to—"

"They found him, Darcy." Luke released the mic on his shoulder. "Farther downstream."

She blinked. "They found him. Is he...?"

"Cuts, bruises. Same as you, I expect." Luke studied her. "But you need to let us examine you and the boy to be sure."

"Daddy!" Brody wailed.

Luke patted his arm. Brody shrank against Darcy. "Your daddy's okay. He's on his way with your uncle Charlie."

Her arms sagged. "He's okay? He's coming?"

Ethan touched her hand. "Darcy, let us help you. Please."

She allowed him to lead her into the open pasture beyond the trees. In the distance, the metal roof of the Savage garden center glimmered. But she didn't let go of Brody, and Brody didn't let go of her.

Lights strobing, an ambulance waited, alongside several SUVs and pickup trucks.

Her limbs shook as the adrenaline exited her body. "H-how did you find us?"

Ethan propelled her toward the open doors of the ambulance. She sat on the tailgate.

"It was too turbulent to get a boat in the water to look for you." Ethan propped his work boot on the fender. "But your dad had everyone between Kiptohanock and Accomac searching seaside."

Her father, the Reverend Harold Parks. There were advantages in being a preacher's kid, she realized. How blessed she was to be the daughter of Harold and Agnes Parks.

Ethan handed her a towel so she could wipe Brody's face. "Sawyer Kole spotted the three of you in the kayak and called it in." An Accomack County patrol cruiser barreled up the farm road toward them. "Speaking of Jax."

Before Deputy Charlie Pruitt could bring the cruiser to a standstill, Jax threw himself out. He ran the remaining distance, bridging the gap between them.

She let go of Brody, who scrambled down. Tears coursing down his face, Jax embraced his son.

The ex-Green Beret soldier buried his face in the wet strands of Brody's hair. Darcy's throat constricted. Jax's shoulders shook.

As he clutched Brody to his chest, Jax's gaze found hers. They shared a long look. His eyes swam with gratitude. A gratitude for so much more than just today. Then Charlie stepped into her line of sight, breaking their visual connection.

Just like that, she knew it was time to go. Jax—and Brody—would be okay without her. For her, the summer had come to an end. It was time to move on to what else God had for her.

The life He had for her elsewhere. A life without Jax and his son. She could almost feel the momentum of the pendulum slowing. Her cue to go before things got awkward. Before the embarrassing, post-climatic pulling back began. Her time with Jax was over.

An unbreachable chasm yawned between them.

Despite the longing surging through her heart, she had to walk away. She'd fulfilled her purpose in their lives this summer, bringing them both to a place of healing. Freeing Jax to pursue a new life with his son. One day, maybe finding love. But with someone else.

Stringing things out only prolonged the inevitable ending she'd seen coming months ago. History had proved she wasn't the kind of woman Jax went for. And she didn't think she could stand by and watch him fall in love with someone else. Or see them make a family with Brody.

Darcy hopped off the ambulance. "Would you take me home, Ethan?"

His blue eyes narrowed. "But what about—"

"Please, Ethan…"

At the pleading note in her voice, he nodded.

She cast one final glance at Jax and Brody, surrounded by the paramedics. Ethan steered her toward his waiting truck.

All those years ago, Jax had been right about not saying goodbye. Darcy didn't know where to even begin saying goodbye to them. So she wouldn't. As she climbed into Ethan's truck, her eyes blurred with unshed tears. It was better this way.

This time, she needed to be the one to leave. But until the day she died, she'd never love anyone the way she loved Jaxon Pruitt and his son.

Chapter Seventeen

Knowing Brody was safe, Jax drew his first even breath. But what about Darcy? Was she okay?

With a strange sense of déjà vu, for the second time that day he looked up to find someone he cared about missing. The open ambulance sat empty.

Cared about? His own lack of honesty smote him. Just as well, though, that Darcy had disappeared. She was probably already en route to Riverside, where Jax and Brody were headed, too. To be poked, prodded and checked for any ill effects from their near fatal encounter with the flash flood.

He'd see her there, but wished he'd had the opportunity to thank her before she was whisked away. To give voice to the gratitude in his heart for all she'd done to save Brody. Without her help, he and Brody might be floating facedown somewhere out at sea.

A sober realization. Except for Darcy and God… He hugged his son.

Brody balked at getting into the ambulance. So they rode in Charlie's patrol car. The paramedics headed off to help others struggling in the storm's aftermath. To Brody's delight, Charlie turned on the siren.

Jax's parents were waiting for them outside the bustling emergency entrance. "How did they—?" He glowered at his brother.

"Don't blame me." Charlie shrugged. "You know Dad still monitors emergency channels on the scanner."

His mother, the retired nurse, insisted on checking their vitals herself. Like the former law enforcement officer he'd once been, his father rapid-fire interrogated Jax regarding the timeline of events.

Arms crossed, Charlie leaned against the doorjamb of the examining room. "If there's trouble to be had, Jax will find it." He smirked.

Jax grimaced, reckoning Darcy might not be off base about the leaning thing. It *was* annoying. As was this unwanted attention.

He shooed away his mother's hands. "I'm fine, Ma."

Groaning, he climbed off the examining table. But he'd survived far worse than this.

Brody held on to Jax's hand while the ER staff made a vain attempt to wash off the grime coating the little boy's face. At the sight of his bedraggled but alive son, Jax blinked away the moisture welling in his eyes. Losing Brody might have proved to be the one thing he wouldn't have survived.

He caught Brody in another hug, inhaling the earthy mixture of mud plus other elements Jax preferred not to contemplate.

"Dawcy?"

"Is she down the hall, Ma?"

She held up two bandages for Brody to choose between. One was lime-green and the other, a neon turquoise. Brody chose green. A heart-wrenching reminder of someone who loved lime-flavored Popsicles. Brody grinned as his grandmother peeled off the adhesive.

Jax's mother smiled, her eyes crinkling. "Band-Aids make every hurt feel better, don't they, Brody?" She ruffled his son's almost dry hair.

"Ma?" Jax inhaled. "Darcy. Which room?"

His mother stripped off her purple gloves. "She's not here. Despite medical advice, she went home."

Jax started for the door, but got a whiff of marsh mud on himself and did an about-face.

His mother straightened. "How about your dad and I take you two home? We'll stay with Brody if you need to check on her." His mom always could read his mind.

"Maybe consider getting a shower first." Charlie fanned the air. "You stink."

"Give Darcy a chance to sort herself out," his mother urged. "I wouldn't want to see anyone until I'd taken a long, hot bath."

Darcy with his son in her arms at the Savage farm had been the most beautiful sight he'd ever beheld. But his mother was right. Unlike the little tomboy he'd known, the grown-up Darcy didn't like being caught out less than perfectly groomed. And the Parkses wouldn't appreciate him tracking in more mud.

Since his cell phone lay at the bottom of the sea, once his parents drove them home, he used the landline to call Darcy. But she didn't pick up, so he left a message for her to call him. Leaving Brody to his adoring grandmother, he made short work of his own restoration. But the phone didn't ring.

"Why don't you eat something?" An enticing aroma arose from the pan his father stirred on the stovetop. "Let her spend the evening recouping with her parents."

"Me hungwy…" Brody padded into the kitchen wrapped in a towel.

Jax's mom trotted after him. "Least we know Brody's feeling fine."

She and his dad laughed, but Jax's heart tugged at him to go check on Darcy. A disquieting urgency filled him. She hadn't returned his call.

But maybe his parents were right. After this morning at the tree house, the Parkses might not exactly lay out the welcome mat for the likes of Jaxon Pruitt.

Perhaps he should give Darcy, all of them, a chance to regain their equilibrium. After all, what was so urgent that he needed to say it now? Tomorrow was another day. Another paddle. Plenty of time to talk before the upcoming Labor Day festivities.

And suppose she stood in front of him right now? What would he say? He scrubbed his hand across his face. Probably better to wait until his heightened emotions had a chance to cool down. Before they crossed a threshold he hadn't yet had time to think through.

He pulled out a chair. "Let's eat."

But his cut-to-the-chase father beat him to the punch. "What do you plan to do about Darcy?" His dad plunked a plate with a fried bologna sandwich in front of Jax.

His mother lifted towel-clad Brody into the booster. "Darcy's leaving in a week, son."

"Wanna cut me a little slack, folks?" He raised both hands. "Considering I just survived a near drowning." He stabbed his fork into a peach slice. "And it's two weeks before she leaves."

At the table, his mother settled into Darcy's customary seat. "I stand corrected."

Jax scowled. Since when did Darcy have a customary seat in his house? Since…since the night he'd moved here, that's when.

His mom cut Brody's sandwich into triangles. "Despite my best efforts, stubborn you've got in spades, my dear firstborn son. A good woman needs to make sure you, Brody Pruitt, don't turn out the same."

Brody grinned from ear to ear, a peach slice where his teeth should have been.

"Stop interfering." Jax threw his fork onto the plate. "I've tried to be clear with Darcy. Let me be as clear with you two. I have no intention of ever marrying again."

Gail Pruitt sucked in her cheeks. "When have we ever interfered in the lives of our children?"

Since the debacle with Anna's first husband? Since their strained relationship with Jax's wife? Although to be fair, that was more Adrienne's doing than theirs.

It was obvious how much they adored Charlie's young wife, Evy. And yes, his folks were practically best friends with the reverend and Miss Agnes. But more than that, Darcy's in-your-face-Jax attitude had tickled his dad since the sandbox days. They loved Darcy.

"Don't take that tone with your mother, Jaxon." His dad didn't raise his voice. He never did, which, as a lawman and father, made it all the more ominous. "You let that girl get away from you once. Don't allow it to happen again."

Jax pushed back from the table, his chair scraping the linoleum.

His mother frowned. "You haven't finished—"

"I'm not hungry."

"But—"

"Let him go, Gail."

On the deck, Jax drew deep lungfuls of air, trying to calm his fraught nerves. But images of Darcy filled his mind. That first summer evening when iridescent bubbles floated around her. Darcy giving chase to Brody, her hair flying free and wild behind her. And despite everything, plunging without hesitation into the woods—and the floodwaters—when his son was lost.

The door creaked open, and he felt his father's ponderous tread on the deck.

"Why won't you allow yourself to love that girl?" His father joined him at the railing. "A girl who's loved you her entire life. And if you were honest with yourself—"

"You're wrong, Dad." He moved away. "I don't love her. I—I can't love her."

"But why, son? Everyone saw this day coming with you two, even if you didn't."

"Everyone?"

"Me, your mom, Darcy's parents. Every brother you've got. Your sister, Darcy's best friend." His father stared over the placid creek. "Your aunt Shirley."

"You set us up," Jax growled. "Taking the business away from Darcy broke her heart."

His father angled his head. "Was it us that broke her heart?"

"No." He bit down on his lip, hard. "I'm the one who did that."

"What we did was give you both the chance to turn the hands of time back a stroke. To explore what might have been. To discover what yet could be."

Jax scrubbed his face with his hand. "She worked her whole life to own the shop, and she hated me for taking it from her."

"She didn't hate you." His father shrugged. "And if nothing had sparked between you, Shirley's backup plan was to open another shop bayside, and give it to Darcy. No one would've been worse for wear. But something did spark between you, didn't it?"

More than sparked. A long-burning ember had burst into flame. Something so sweet. After Adrienne's death, something he'd dared not dream of for himself.

"Something I don't deserve."

His dad shook his head. "There's the thing I suspected. Misplaced guilt."

"I'm not the man you think I am." Jax's voice quavered. "I failed Adrienne. I failed my son. The friends I couldn't save." His arm swept the tranquil night. "How do you come back from that?"

His father laid his hand on Jax's shoulder. "I've never experienced combat. But as a deputy, I witnessed things… I had to do things that were hard. And only one thing ever gave me peace."

Jax swallowed. "I can't remember what peace feels like, Dad."

"There's only one source of peace, son. Jesus said to come to Him when we're weary. He promises to take the heavy load off our shoulders and place it on His own. And in laying down our burdens, we find true rest in Him."

A burden-bearer, Reverend Harold had said.

Jax hung his head. "How do I lay it down, Dad?"

"It starts with forgiveness. And forgiveness includes forgiving yourself." His father exhaled. "Didn't mean to get preachy. I usually leave that stuff to the reverend."

"The reverend is a smart man."

His father gave Jax a faint smile. "I'm better with sirens and handcuffs. But you're not as alone as you feel, son." The tough ex-lawman's eyes gleamed. "God is always there, right beside us. As close as a prayer."

"I hear you, Dad. I do."

"Your mom and I should get home." His bear of a father grabbed Jax into a hug. "Never forget how much we love you. We're praying for you, too."

Later, standing at the foot of Brody's small bed, Jax watched the steady rise and fall of his son's chest as he slept. This day could have ended so differently. So tragically. God was good.

He remembered what Charlie had told him at the beginning of the summer. Was it true that God caused everything to work out for good for those who loved Him?

Jax headed downstairs. Outside the window, a yellowish light blinked on and off. Drawn by the display, he moved once again to the deck. Was peace possible for someone like him?

After being lost for so long, he'd found his way home to Kiptohanock. But he couldn't fathom how God could make something good out of the mess he'd made of his life thus far.

Despite the so-called Pruitt charm, he wasn't good in the romance department. His failure with Adrienne only underscored his inability to sustain a long-term relationship. His friendship with Darcy was the only relationship with a woman he'd ever managed not to destroy.

Loving Darcy was the easy part. Okay. He was ready to admit it—typical—when it was too late to do anything about it. Perhaps that was his real problem—he deliberately left things too late, self-sabotaging.

A day late and a dollar short. Though she might not see herself as maternal, Darcy was the perfect mother for Brody. And Jax's heart kept insisting she'd be the perfect wife for him.

The problem was he was no good for her. He'd hurt her, just like he'd hurt his wife. He'd fail Darcy—just like he failed Adrienne. That was the part he couldn't face—hurting Darcy. Other than Brody, she was the best thing in his life. And he'd rather die than hurt her.

"God, I love her so much…" His voice was a ragged sob. "She deserves so much more than a broken, messed-up excuse of a man like me."

She deserved so much more than he could ever give. She deserved somebody like Ethan… Jax's breath hitched, his stomach cramping. Someone with no baggage. Someone who would love her the way she deserved to be loved.

Jax clenched his jaw. He needed to love her enough to do the right thing and let her go. Once and for all. As long as he and Brody kept hanging around, she'd never find her perfect guy.

He squeezed his eyes shut. Jax wanted to be her perfect guy. The idea of someone else courting Darcy, right under his nose… Marrying her, starting a family with her…

Jax's heart tore in two. Could he stand by and watch that unfold before his eyes? Yet what other option was there?

There could be no future with Darcy until the issues of the past had been resolved. The guilt he bore over Adrienne weighed him down, a boulder lodged on his shoulders. And he was being crushed. Like finding himself underwater, trapped beneath an overturned kayak. Drowning as surely as he'd almost drowned in the creek earlier.

His father's words floated like a whisper on the

breeze. *Come...* Was it that easy? Giving God the guilt, and in exchange, receiving peace?

Jax gripped the railing, the splintered wood rough against his palms. And was reminded of the yoke of the cross. Not easy, but hard. The cost of Jax's peace.

"Help me, God. Forgive me for the wrong I've done to You, and Adrienne. Help me to let go of the guilt. I can't bear it any longer. I never could. Please grant Your peace and rest to me. A peace and rest I'll never find apart from You."

The night was quiet, except for the clicking song of the cicadas. Down in the marsh, the croaking bass of the frogs. But he felt lighter, the sorrow lifting.

Fireflies flitted from one edge of the forest to the other. Like his guilt, drifting away until lost from sight. The scent of honeysuckle permeated the night air. And for the first time in two years, he felt able to draw a deep, clean breath.

The best word in the universe forgiven. No matter what the future held with Darcy, he'd hang on to God's peace. But he needed to make something else right, too.

Jax dialed his aunt Shirley in Florida for an overdue conversation. Then he headed to bed. His rest was undisturbed. The best he'd slept in years.

He awoke to beams of sunlight dancing on the ceiling. As he swung his legs over the side of the bed, the peace he'd experienced last night remained. And something more—freedom. A freedom found in forgiveness, enabling Jax to say the next best word in the universe. A word meant only for Darcy.

Love.

Chapter Eighteen

Unable to wait any longer, he roused a sleepy-eyed Brody. Too wired to eat breakfast, Jax made a quick phone call to his parents.

He was the kind of guy who just needed a plan. And he liked to call this latest plan the Wooing and Winning of Darcy Parks. He couldn't keep from smiling. His plan, if he did say so, was perfect.

Item one—drop Brody off at his mom's and walk over to Darcy's house.

But when he pulled into the Pruitt driveway, he noticed Darcy's SUV was missing next door. He frowned at this obvious wrinkle. But maybe she'd gone on a Long John run for her dad. The reverend did love those cinnamon, powder-dusted pastries. She'd probably be home soon.

He toted Brody to the Pruitt house. On the porch, he set his son on his feet. His mother yanked open the door.

"You have no idea how happy I am to see you, son." She waved at Brody. "We'll have a grand time together." She arched an eyebrow at Jax. "Take your time. All the time you need."

He drew a deep breath. Somehow his mom always knew exactly what was going on with him. She closed the door after Brody trundled inside.

Jax squared his shoulders. He would beg Darcy's forgiveness, eat as much crow as she served. Which he deserved. After their phone conversation last night, Shirley had emailed the document. The printed out paper—signing Kiptohanock Kayaking over to Darcy Parks—crinkled in the pocket of his cargo shorts.

Then the next phase of his plan—to get on his knee. His lips quirked. Maybe in the tree house? And beg her to marry him, changing Darcy Parks to Darcy Pruitt. The plan was simplicity itself. Genius.

Jax threaded his way through the crepe myrtles, then paused midstep. Her SUV was still gone. But no matter. Per Southern tradition, he ought to talk with her father first, anyway.

His shoes crunching the shell gravel, Jax strode toward the Parks backyard. The backyard where Shore folks did their living. And proposing. Passing the oak tree, he grinned, his anticipation mounting.

Jax took the steps to the screened porch in a single bound. The hinges of the door squeaked as he pulled it open. He'd raised his fist to knock when the reverend swung open the storm door.

Startled, Jax blinked. The reverend didn't look so good. There were bags under his eyes, and he looked older than Jax remembered seeing him. Was he ill? Or was Miss Agnes? Perhaps Darcy had gone to the drugstore for medicine.

But like the ex-Green Beret operative he was, Jax rallied to the unexpected. He cleared his throat. "Sir, if I could have a brief word with you?"

The reverend swiped his hand over his face. "Is this about my daughter?"

Jax went into parade formation, arms at his sides, posture straight. "I'd like to ask for your daughter's hand in marriage, sir."

Silence.

"I'd like your permission to ask Darcy to marry me, sir." As if the reverend had another daughter besides Darcy.

An inexplicable sadness lined his face. "She's not here, Jaxon."

The plan wasn't unfolding as expected, but he'd been trained to adapt to changing conditions. "With your permission, sir, I'll wait." He gestured toward the tree house.

"You don't understand, Jaxon. She's gone."

His heart hammered. "When will she be back?"

"We love you, son, and we always hoped…" Harold Parks looked away. "But she's not coming back, Jaxon. She left first thing this morning for Florida."

A roaring filled his head. Surely he'd misheard Darcy's dad.

"She wasn't supposed to leave for two weeks."

"I'm sorry, Jaxon." Her father touched his arm. "She came home yesterday afternoon and packed her bags. She phoned Chas to make sure you wouldn't be left in the lurch during the busy Labor Day weekend."

A lurch was exactly what he was in without her. A lurch that had nothing to do with kayaking. Jax scrubbed his neck.

This couldn't be happening. She couldn't be gone. Not after everything they'd shared. Not after everything they meant to each other.

Not when all the unspoken promises might finally come true between them. *God...where are You in this?*

"When did she leave?"

"First light. We tried to get her to reconsider. But she was determined to go."

Taking a page from the Jaxon Pruitt playbook. He winced. Leaving without saying goodbye. Leaving unanswered the question he hadn't had the chance to ask.

Not true. Nausea roiled in his belly. A question he'd had years to ask, but hadn't.

"She's gone..." Maybe if he said it out loud, he'd come closer to accepting it.

Harold squeezed his arm. "By now she's probably on the mainland, heading south."

Jax blanked out the next few minutes. His plan—the not-so-perfect plan—had fallen apart. He stumbled away, and found himself in the Pruitt kitchen.

From the living room, a children's show blared from the television. With Brody occupied, in short, clipped sentences, he told his parents what had happened next door. And what hadn't.

"Go after her," his mother urged.

"I think I already did that when I came back to Kiptohanock." His chest squeezed. "Her response is clear. And this time, final."

His father's face clouded. "I'm sorry, son. Let Brody spend the day with us. You need some time to yourself."

Dazed, Jax nodded. He should check on the part-timers at the store. Best to keep busy. As for processing the loss of Darcy? He had a feeling he'd be grappling with that for a long, long time.

His mom wrapped her arms around him. "A son never gets too big for a hug."

Stooping, for a second he rested his head on her shoulder. "This son never gets too big to need a hug."

His dad pursed his lips. "We'll bring Brody to your house after supper."

At the shop, Jax sent Savannah on the new winery paddle. Ozzie headed up a clamming trip. Business was brisk. His ideas and Darcy's know-how were paying off. They made—his gut twisted—had made a great team.

He kept close to the store. But when Chas arrived to lead the sunset paddle, Jax went home.

The house was dark. Empty and soulless without Brody. He drifted from room to room, restless, consumed with grief.

Until the gently lapping water called him outside. For better or worse, he was a born here. Meant to live his life within sight and sound of the water. It was who Jax was in the deepest part of himself.

Out on the water, perhaps he'd find solace. Pour out his heart to God. Find a way to make peace with the hole Darcy's leaving left in his heart.

He glided out from the bank. His strokes smooth and even, he pushed himself, punishing himself, until his shoulders ached and he came to the end of his strength.

Resting the paddle across his lap, he closed his eyes. Praying for wisdom. For courage. For Darcy, wherever she was.

The kayak drifted, borne along by the swell of the incoming tide. He'd been drifting ever since Adrienne died. But here he'd found safe harbor. Because of Darcy.

With her, he'd glimpsed the possibility of truly coming home. Without her, his mooring had been torn away. And when Brody realized yet another person he loved was never coming back…?

Jax closed his eyes, his chin sinking onto his chest. Would the gains he'd made with Brody be undone? His son would need him now more than ever. And Jax would be there for him, whatever it took, no matter the cost. He wouldn't let Brody down.

But for now, he needed to get his act together. Find the courage to go on without Darcy. Take hold of the strength that could only come from God.

Stilling his heart, he shut down the mushrooming panic. Quieted the clamoring images of what would never be.

The screech of a seagull echoed across the salt marsh. Jax inhaled, releasing the breath slowly through his lips. His senses drank in the sounds and sensations around him. The plink of water dripping off the end of his paddle. The feel of the current against the kayak.

Yielding to the pull of the tide, he floated on the water, surrendering his will to the One who'd always loved him the most and best. Despite Jax's inability to see Him. Or his stubborn refusal to acknowledge Him.

Peace soaked through the pain piercing his heart. Time to go home. To his son and the life they'd have to create without Darcy.

Taking up the paddle, he turned the kayak.

Dusk had fallen. He rounded the bend, expecting to find his home ablaze with lights, with his parents and Brody. But the house remained dark.

His stroke quickened. Where were they? Had something happened? He sliced through the water.

Jax drove the kayak onto the beach. He leaped out, the water cold against his ankles. As cold as the sudden fear gripping him.

He dragged the boat above the waterline and came up the incline at a run. It was then he spotted the tiny pinpricks of light. The yellowish, greenish sparks skimming the blades of grass. Flitting through the branches of the trees. Hovering above the creek. Everywhere.

At a rush of movement, he spotted his son. Zigzagging, Brody reached for the sky as he ran. Chasing the elusive lights.

"Daddy! Whitening bugs." His childish laughter floated across the yard.

Lightning bugs. And behind Brody, another figure. In her hands, a canning jar glowed with fireflies.

Jax's throat closed.

"Hello, Jax."

The flickering light illuminated her eyes. And in her gaze, he beheld a vulnerable uncertainty.

Jax found his voice. "Long time no see, Darce."

Her lips curving, she held out the jar. "We're catching fireflies."

"So I see."

"I got to North Carolina before I turned around." She broke eye contact, searching for Brody. Following the sound of his laughter.

"Why did you turn around, Darcy?"

"It occurred to me the lightning bugs would be gone soon. And I couldn't let summer end—" her voice wobbled "—without showing Brody the fireflies."

Brody dashed over. "Wook, Daddy."

A firefly had landed on his arm. Brody giggled as it tickled his skin. A glow pulsed from the tail end of the bug, and his son's eyes grew large.

"Cool, Brode."

Opening its wings, the firefly lifted off and flew into the night. Brody gave chase.

Darcy thrust the jar at Jax. "We're having a contest to see who can catch the most." Holes had been punched in the lid.

"What does the winner get?" His voice went husky.

A vein fluttered in the sweet hollow of her throat. "What do you want to win, Jax?"

"You." He handed the wrinkled paper to her.

"What's this?"

"I'll file the official forms at the courthouse, but I'm signing the business over to you."

Her mouth rounded. "What? Why, Jax?"

"Because it's rightfully yours."

"Kiptohanock Kayaking belongs to you, Jax. It's your new start with Brody."

He brought her hand to his lips. "There is no life here for me without you. There is no home without you in it." His voice cracked.

"Jax…"

"You, Darcy Parks, are the great love of my life. Marry me, Darce." He gulped. "Please."

Jaxon Pruitt loved her.

"I—I haven't lost you, have I?" he stammered, so unlike the ever confident, slightly arrogant Jax she'd known since childhood.

Everything faded for Darcy. There was only Jax and her. In his eyes, a longing she could scarcely comprehend. A longing for her.

"I went to the tree this morning, but you were gone. It's been a bad day, Darce," he whispered. "Believing you were gone forever. Thinking I'd missed my chance—again—to tell you how much I love you."

"You love me…" Her voice held a note of awe, as if she couldn't quite believe it was true.

He sighed. "I planned this whole thing to take place at our tree."

It had somehow always been their tree.

She pressed her lips together to keep them from trembling. "You and your plans, Jax."

Hands cupped, Brody ran over to them. The

black-winged creature flashed in the cradle of his palms. "Dawcy! Daddy!"

Jax's brow furrowed. "I think it's time to let the fireflies go."

She blinked. "Let them go? Why, Jax?"

"No, Daddy!" Brody hugged his firefly to his chest. "Me catched them. Mine. They bewong to me."

"That's what I used to think." Jax shook his head. "But the fireflies don't belong to us. They belong to God."

"No, Daddy. God not want my whitening bugs."

Jax laced his fingers, warm and strong, with Darcy's. "They were given to us not to keep, but to enjoy for just a little while."

Goose bumps pebbled her skin. He wasn't talking about lightning bugs. Her heart pounded.

"Now it's time to release them back to God, Who loves them more than we could ever imagine."

Jax's words weren't for Brody. His words were for her.

"The past, with its mistakes and regrets." His gaze locked on to hers. "The pain."

Brody's lips poked out. "Me can't, Daddy."

Handing her the jar, Jax squeezed Brody's shoulder. "Yes, you can, my son. For the sake of our new life. A new love." Jax's dark eyes swallowed Darcy whole. "We can because we must."

A new life. For the sake of a new love… Her father had understood what she had not. His first family wasn't lost.

"We'll release them together." Her gaze shot to Jax. "I'll help you, if you want me to."

"I want *you*." Reaching out, he tucked a tendril of hair behind her ear. "But your dreams matter, Darce. If Florida is where your heart lies—"

"My heart lies with you, Jaxon Pruitt." She touched Brody's cheek. "And with your son."

"*Our* son." Jax's mouth trembled. "God has given us the gift of making a life for him." Then Jax bit his lip. "I mean… You never said… Does that mean yes?"

"I love you, Jax." She fingered the cleft in his chin. "Yes, I'll marry you." She smiled through a blur of tears. "I'll marry you both." She cupped his jaw.

Drawing her close, he took a deep breath. As if somehow he'd been afraid she wouldn't marry him. Or love him.

"I love you so much." He pressed his lips to her palm. "I hope you won't get tired of hearing me say that."

She smiled into his hand. "I won't get tired." A whiff of his sandalwood aftershave teased her nostrils, curling her toes.

Brody raised the jar. "Fuwst count."

"One, two, three…" She let go of Jax to tick off the number of bugs crawling inside the glass.

"Me thwee."

Darcy hugged Brody's neck. "Not quite. Not yet."

Jax peered at the jar in Brody's hands. "Four, five, six…"

"Seben, ate…ten!" Brody grinned.

Jax caught her eye. "We'll keep working on his numbers."

"Me win!" Brody fist-pumped the air.

"I'm the one who wins." While Brody did a happy dance, Jax set her dangly earring in motion with his fingertip. "How does Mr. and Mrs. Pruitt of Kiptohanock Kayaking sound to you?"

"Great." She pursed her lips. "But what would you think of spending winters in the Keys?"

"An adventurous life." He slid his arm around her waist. "I love it."

Life with Jax Pruitt promised to be more than adventurous. It promised to be glorious.

Darcy fluttered her lashes. "Maybe we could even throw in a treasure-hunting scuba dive in the Caribbean."

"I like the way you think." He looked at her. "But always, there'll be summers in Kiptohanock."

Was this really happening? To her, Darcy Parks, the PK from Kiptohanock, Virginia? *Thank You, God…for dreams come true.*

Jax smiled at her in that half-lidded, ridiculously stomach-quivering way of his. "By the way… " he jerked his thumb at the house "…I've got a box of lime-green freezer pops waiting for you."

Her happiness felt a mile wide and as tall as their tree. "My favorite."

"Mine, too. I think I'm also going to build a tree house here." He winked. "For convenience sake, of course."

"And a swing." Tears pricked her eyes. "Brody would love that."

"He's not the only one." Jax wound a strand of her hair around his finger. "I've always kind of had a thing for redheads, Darce."

"I'm not a—"

"One redhead in particular."

Her heart turned over. "Oh."

She knelt beside Brody. "Did you say goodbye to the lightning bugs, Brody?"

Crouching, Jax heard his knees crack. "Such fragile, beautiful creatures." He sighed. "Here for such a short time."

She knew he was thinking of someone else, but Darcy no longer felt insecure about what Jax had shared with Adrienne. The past had ultimately made him a better man. And there was Brody. For him, Darcy would forever be grateful.

After kissing her palm, Jax held her hand against his jaw. "But oh, the joy they bring to us."

She wasn't second choice or a runner-up in Jax's heart. What they had with each other was for them alone. New. Complete. Enough. Like the family her father had created with Darcy's mom.

Tears slid down her cheeks. "It will be okay, Brody." Jax swam before her vision. "There's always next summer."

"As many summers as God allows." His voice deepened. "I love you, Darcy. I always have."

Her heart soared. Because this time…this time she was sure he meant it. She could trust Jax with her heart, her dreams, with everything.

"I love you, too, Jax."

Brody nudged them. "'Kay, Daddy. I'm weddy." He held on to the bottom of the jar while Jax unscrewed the lid.

Darcy rose. "Make a wish, Brody. Say a prayer."

Standing, Jax wrenched off the lid. Brody swirled the jar until the fireflies flew out.

His face puckered. "Me woozing them, Dawcy. They gone, Daddy."

"They're not gone forever, Brody." She pointed to the indigo sky. "Come next summer, the fireflies will be right where you let them go."

Leaning, Jax draped his arm around her shoulders. She smiled. The man couldn't stand up straight to save his life, but he was exactly where he should be. Next to her.

He pressed Brody against them. "They're headed home, son."

She swallowed, thinking of the half brother she'd never met. Yet… "And nothing's ever truly lost if you know where to find it."

Jax picked up Brody, and she hugged them both.

Something passed over Jax's features. "When I feel your arms around me, Darcy, I know I'm home."

"Me, too," she whispered.

In the longing for home, a yearning as old as the human heart. A place where "goodbye" need never again be said. A place of hello, a place of welcome, a place of grace.

They exchanged a long, slow look before lifting their gazes to the sky. And they watched the blinking flashes of the fireflies, floating ever upward. Going home. Becoming one with the star-studded summer night on the banks of the tidal creek.

* * * * *

If you loved this tale of sweet romance,
pick up these other stories
from author Lisa Carter

COAST GUARD COURTSHIP
COAST GUARD SWEETHEART
FALLING FOR THE SINGLE DAD
THE DEPUTY'S PERFECT MATCH
THE BACHELOR'S UNEXPECTED FAMILY
THE CHRISTMAS BABY

Available now from Love Inspired!

Find more great reads at
www.LoveInspired.com

Dear Reader,

Like Jax, have you ever struggled with guilt? Which have you found harder—to forgive someone else or to forgive yourself? Neither are easy.

Or like Darcy, have you ever felt second best or second choice?

But when Darcy embraces the person God made her to be and pursues the dreams God placed in her heart, only then does she gain real freedom and peace. Whatever dream God has placed in your heart, I pray you, too, will find the courage to pursue it.

Whenever you're feeling second choice, read Isaiah 43 to see how much God loves you. He has redeemed you and called you by name. You have a place all your own in God's heart. You have been chosen—you are His.

And what about dealing with guilt? True guilt drives us to repentance and helps us find our way back to what is right. False guilt, however, brings only condemnation, with no way out. True guilt leading to repentance brings freedom and healing. False guilt paralyses and enslaves.

This is a heavy burden we were never created to shoulder. Jesus took the heavy load of sin on the cross so that you don't have to. He is the only one who can be our burden-bearer. It is in the laying down of our burdens that we find rest and peace in Him. I hope you will accept His invitation to come so that you, too, might experience true freedom, healing and restoration.

May we all find the strength to finally accept what is past, to fully embrace the present and to look to the future with hope-filled eyes.

Thank you for allowing me in this series of books to share with you a very special place and people dear to my heart on the Eastern Shore of Virginia.

I hope you have enjoyed taking this journey with me, Brody, Darcy and Jax. I would love to hear from you. You may email me at lisa@lisacarterauthor.com or visit www.lisacarterauthor.com.

Wishing you fair winds and following seas,

Lisa Carter